The Friday Night DATE DRESS

talena winters

My Secret Wish PUBLISHING

Published by My Secret Wish Publishing
www.mysecretwishpublishing.com
Contact the author at talena@talenawinters.com

ISBN (print, revised edition): 978-1-989800-02-7
ISBN (eBook): 978-0-9947364-1-3

Cover and Title Page design by Talena Winters
First edition edited by Lora Doncea, editsbylora.com
Author Photo: Amanda Monette. Used with permission.

Synopsis: A brokenhearted diner waitress works through her grief by sewing couture dresses. She is befriended by an aspiring photographer looking for his lucky break who only wants to see her smile. His meddling sister might be the only thing standing between these two and what they both need.

To my parents,
who taught me to love stories.

To my husband,
who gave me a love story.

Chapter 1

MELINDA DROPPED HER KEYS and purse on the kitchen counter and closed the door of her tiny one-bedroom suite. She kicked off her work shoes and sighed in relief as her throbbing feet sank gratefully into the hall carpet.

It had been a typical Thursday working at the diner. Truck drivers, cops, and local shop owners kept her running all day, every one of them lousy tippers. She wondered why Sandra never complained about her tips—but then, with her fluffy blond hair, doe eyes, and flirtatious smile, she was probably collecting tips just for showing up at a guy's table.

Melinda paused to glance in the mirror by the door at her own features, then turned away. She knew what she would see—dark hair pulled back in a messy pony tail, tired grey eyes, a mouth set in a firm line. It had been years since she could smile at all, much less produce one like the dazzler Sandra flashed more often than cameras at a wedding.

Her perpetual melancholy drove her boss, Fred, crazy.

"Myers, you gotta smile," he had snapped again that morning. "No one wants to be served by a waitress who looks like she'd rather bite 'em than feed 'em."

"Sorry, Fred," she said. "I thought I *was* smiling."

"Really? Show me."

Melinda forced out the smile she wore for the customers.

"You gotta be kidding me. Looks more like you just ate your dirty laundry. Listen, keep chasing away the customers with your attitude, you're through here, ya hear me?"

Melinda nodded, wide-eyed, scooped up an order of fish and chips from the pass-through, and fled to the dining room. Seriously? She would be fired because she couldn't muster a smile? What about her hard work and accuracy with orders? *And I have never 'chased away a customer.' I get the same people every week. Mostly. Humph.*

Still smarting with the memory, she looked back into her hall mirror with its chipped lacquer frame and put on the same smile she had shown Fred earlier. He was right—there were more sincere smiles on a used car lot. She tried rearranging her muscles to produce something more authentic. No success.

Melinda let out a snort of frustration and made her way to the bathroom to change, brushing past the floor-to-ceiling cardboard boxes stuffed into the tiny living room that blocked out any view of downtown Calgary. Not much to see, anyway—just someone else's windows across the street. She carefully hung her gaudy pale blue-and-white diner uniform with its too-cute frilly apron on a peg behind the door, then threw on the same jeans and black Henley top she had already worn two nights in a row. They still smelled fresh enough, and she wasn't trying to impress anyone, anyway.

Melinda leaned on the kitchen counter and munched on a carrot stick. The microwave hummed behind her with a small Styrofoam cup of soup on its turnstile. She twisted her engagement ring while she waited, caught herself in the nervous habit, and forced her hands to stillness by planting them on the counter. Soon. Soon she'd be in her happy place.

Next to the counter sat a small round dining table completely covered in sewing paraphernalia. Wedged into the space between the table and the wall of dress boxes in the living room stood a linen-covered mannequin. A half-finished dress hung on the mannequin, calling to her with the allure of a mythical siren. She resisted long enough to slurp down the soup, toss the container in the garbage, and splash water on her hands and mouth. Drifting past the table, she stood in front of the dress, which was a vision in grey and black and pink. After a moment caressing the edgy skulls-and-roses silk crepe, she set to work.

It would be the wee hours of the morning before she finally crawled into bed—exhausted, but triumphant—with the completed dress hanging from the top corner of her bedroom door. A smudged pencil sketch of the design was attached to the front, like a seal declaring its finished state. Before she drifted off to sleep, she gave the gown one final, satisfied glance.

Yep, Robert would love it.

"MELINDA-HONEY, would you take table eight? I want to go on my break soon," Sandra drawled as she floated by with a tray of drinks.

Melinda nodded at the blonde woman and fished in her apron for a pen and pad as she crossed the checkered floor.

The couple at table eight were more interested in chatting than reading menus. Hearing their playful, affectionate banter, the familiar twinge of pain pinched her chest, but she suppressed it and tried out the new version of her smile.

Even from her side of her face, she knew it was weak.

"Hi," she said to the tops of their heads during a break in the conversation. "Can I start you with something to drink?"

The dark-haired, mocha-skinned woman who glanced up and met her eye actually made her catch her breath a little. Women that beautiful rarely came into Fred's Diner. Okay, never.

"Iced tea, please," the woman said in a throaty voice.

Melinda jotted down the woman's order. She didn't need to write it down, not really—but she did need an excuse not to stare at the woman. East Indian, she thought, from both the clipped, succinct accent and the way the woman reminded her of the actress on a Bollywood movie poster she saw every day on the way to work.

The man finally looked up. "Make that two."

Melinda dropped her pen.

If the woman's looks made her catch her breath, the man's made her forget that she knew how to breathe at all. Bottomless black eyes, black hair, perfect teeth, a dimple—it was just not fair for that much beauty to be sitting at one table. The man could have been on the Bollywood poster right next to his companion.

Melinda nodded mutely at his order, scooped up her pen from the floor, and fled back behind the counter. Her face burned right up to the top of her head.

What would Robert think of her? *Acting like a*

schoolgirl!

She continued to berate herself as she filled two glasses with ice and sweetened tea from the fountain, and then popped in lemon wedges and straws. By the time she had the drinks on a tray, she had herself thoroughly in hand. She managed to barely tremble when she placed the iced teas on the table in front of one of the most attractive couples she had ever seen. She took their meal orders and served them without further humiliating herself.

After they finished eating, Melinda returned to the table to collect the plates. Oddly, the man was observing her movements with a penetrating stare. She locked her gaze on the dishes, stacking the empty plates in one hand and grabbing the glasses with the other.

"Refill?" She kept her gaze on the table, not daring to meet their eyes.

The man spoke this time. "Yes, please. And I think we'll have some of your mud pie for dessert."

"Oh, Peter. Really? I can't eat that!" The woman looked mortified and pleased at the same time.

Melinda looked at the tiny woman—who could certainly afford a little pie—then thought guiltily of her own meagre portion sizes. *Like I can talk!*

"Preeti, it's not every day that we get to celebrate you landing your dream job! I'll share it with you. You can have a few bites, can't you?"

The woman hesitated.

"Chocolate. Chocolate. Chocolate," Peter chanted.

Finally, she grinned and nodded. "Okay, just a bit."

Peter turned to Melinda. "My sister is the new fashion editor at *Fresh* magazine," he said. "This is our celebration date."

Not a couple, then. Brother and sister. Melinda felt a little flush of heat creep out of her collar.

"Not every girl is lucky enough to have her brother take her to a truck stop for a date," Preeti teased. Then she gasped and looked up at Melinda. "No offense."

"None taken," Melinda replied, surprised to find herself with a small but real smile on her face. It felt so unusual that she stood there, enjoying the sensation for several moments.

She was still standing there, smiling stupidly, when Preeti spoke up.

"So . . . the mud pie? I guess we'll take one after all."

"Oh! Sorry! Of course. I'll be right back with it." She hurried away, the heat wave overtaking her face completely.

Who knew a simple smile could be so much trouble?

Chapter 2

PREETI SHOOK HER HEAD at the waitress's retreating back.

"That girl is a little odd," she said in a low voice. "Too bad she doesn't take better care of herself. She could be quite attractive."

"Well, her fiancé obviously has different standards than you do. You saw the ring, right?"

Peter had glanced at the pretty waitress's left hand out of Single Guy Reflex, and felt a twinge of disappointment to see the fourth finger encircled with a gold band sporting a sizeable diamond. He knew his older sister—who missed no attire detail on anyone in the room—would have seen it, too. Her nod confirmed it. And how high were his sister's standards anyway? This girl might not win pageants, but she was pretty enough, in a classical sort of way.

His girlfriend Anise's face flashed into his mind,

her fiery red hair falling in waves to her shoulders, and he fidgeted with his cutlery. *Old habits die hard, I guess.*

The ponytailed waitress whisked back to their table with iced tea refills and a layered chocolate dessert on a plate. She set everything down, along with two forks, and left without a word.

Peter grabbed his fork and then caught the expression on Preeti's face. He froze and narrowed his eyes.

Peter knew that look all too well. It was the one Preeti wore when she was about to meddle in his life—for his own good, of course. He had experienced the repercussions of her *helping* more often than he cared to remember.

He opened his mouth to stop her, but she spoke quickly.

"I wonder if they have hired their wedding photographer yet?" Preeti indicated the waitress with her fork, then shaved off a small bite of mocha ice cream and slid it into her mouth. Her eyes grew wide. "Oh, this is *good.*" Her words were muffled. "You've got to try this, Peter."

Peter gave her a look of mock exasperation, both for her meddling and his I-told-you-so. "You can ask her, if you're so interested."

He took his own mouthful of chocolate heaven.

She put up her hands in self-defence. "Hey, if you don't start making money as a photographer soon, you'll never be able to take me somewhere nicer than a diner for lunch." She slid the plate closer to her and scooped up a large portion of the dessert.

"Not all of us have hit the big time yet, sis. But I'm working on it." He glanced out the window. "Being a delivery truck driver may not be glamorous, but it pays the bills."

"Oh, Daddy must be so proud. His son the engineer, pinching his pennies as a UPS driver."

"Stop eating my head. You know I don't want to be an engineer, any more than I want to drive that truck for the rest of my life, *didi*." The Hindi word for *older sister* dripped with sarcasm, a reminder that they were not children in Mumbai anymore.

"*You* know that I'm just teasing, little brother." She flashed a bright smile before scooping up another huge bite.

Peter scowled and aimed his fork at the dessert, surprised that his sister had already consumed most of it. He glanced up at Preeti, who was licking off her fork with relish. She looked over at him in mid-lick and he shook his head, eyebrows lifting in amusement.

"'A few bites,' my butt!" He smirked, pulling the plate out of her reach to finish the last few bites himself.

"Oo, look who is learning the local slang!" she said, and then tried to scrape up a little more chocolate from across the table.

Peter curled his arm protectively around the plate and fended off her fork with his other hand, glaring at Preeti in mock outrage at her tenacity.

"Never you mind," she scolded against his silent reproof, but set down her fork with obvious effort, looking chastened.

He shook his head again, chuckling, and quickly finished the last bite during the cease-fire.

Preeti watched him enjoy the final bit of ice cream cake in consternation, then got back to her point.

"Seriously, Peter, you are a very talented photographer, you just need to promote yourself more. You need to get a proper portfolio put together. I want to be able to hire you at *Fresh*, but I'll need to show them something more than snapshots of our friends on Facebook to prove that you know what you're doing."

"I will get to it, Preeti. Stop eating my head!" he exclaimed again, but he maintained his teasing grin—with effort.

"When?" Preeti asked, steely gaze holding his.

Peter was saved from responding when the waitress flew up to their table on her thick-soled white sneakers. She wiped her hands on her apron before speaking. Her eyes focused on the blue Formica tabletop, not them.

"Can I get you anything else?"

"Yes, actually," Preeti replied, giving Peter a meaningful glare and then turning toward the waitress with a gracious, well-practised smile. She ducked her head until the girl was forced to look at her, though she seemed to do so only begrudgingly.

"My brother here is a talented photographer, and I can vouch that he is quite good at what he does. He's too shy to ask, but he was wondering if you have already hired your wedding photographer."

Peter shot darts at his sister with his eyes.

She ignored him.

The girl winced. "Wedding photographer?"

She started twirling the ring on her finger with her left thumb and bit her lower lip, her eyes suddenly moist. "Um, no, we haven't. My, uh, fiancé, Robert, he's a pilot. He's gone a lot, so we haven't had time to work out a lot of the details yet."

Peter couldn't make sense of her reaction, but he weighed his options. Starting his photography career with a wedding was enough to make his insides curdle, but he knew Preeti was right. There was no time like the present. If his older sister—who rarely wasted compliments—believed he could do a wedding, then maybe he could.

"Peter." He thrust his hand toward the waitress.

She hesitated, then took it.

"And this is Preeti, my sister." He nodded toward Preeti. "Uh . . ." he squinted at her name tag,

"Melinda. May I borrow your pen?"

The girl handed it over, and he scribbled his name and phone number on a napkin. He gave it to her, and she stared at the scrawl in black ink.

"I'd love to be your photographer, if you are interested." He infused as much confidence as he could muster into his voice and ignored the smug look he caught on Preeti's face out of the corner of his eye. "Give me a call, and we can get together when it works best for you. I'll show you some of my stuff."

He hesitated, chagrined at his own nerve.

What stuff? Landscapes and bumblebees?

"Well, what I've got so far, anyway. Photography isn't my full-time gig—yet—but I am . . . working on it. I'm usually off work by about five-thirty."

He jerked his thumb at the cube delivery truck visible through the window, as if the tan-and-brown uniform he was wearing weren't explanation enough. He did a mental face-palm. *Way to work the sales pitch, bro.*

"I get off then, too," Melinda said. She seemed a bit dazed as she folded the napkin and tucked it into her apron. "Uh, thanks, P-Peter. I . . . I will. I'll give you a call."

She dropped the bill on the table between them, gathered up their dirty dishes, and was gone from their table faster than rain seeping into the dry, cracked Indian soil at the beginning of monsoon.

"Strange girl," Preeti mused. She shrugged. "I guess it takes all kinds."

"It *does*. Doesn't it?"

Peter aimed the comment toward his sister, who did not look the least bit embarrassed by her audacity. He shook his head. She'd never been embarrassed by it before. Why would he expect her to start now?

As Peter sipped the last of his iced tea, he watched Melinda scurry around the diner as though she were on autopilot. She did her job thoroughly and efficiently, but without an ounce of joy.

Maybe she was having a bad day. But he sensed not.

"I think she's lonely," he said, mostly to himself.

"Lonely?" Preeti followed his gaze. "She's engaged!"

Melinda was taking an order from the booth two down from theirs. Every mannerism seemed to declare that unnecessary interaction was not welcome.

Preeti pursed her lips. "Well, maybe. Maybe the ring is some form of defence against unwanted attention. Some waitresses do that, you know, so guys like you don't hit on her. Maybe she's not engaged at all. And don't you have a girlfriend? Denise something?"

"Anise," Peter corrected her. "I'm . . . not hitting on her. You were, remember?"

Preeti gave him a smug smile. "And now you have a potential photography client. You're welcome."

Peter frowned. He remembered the odd look Melinda had given him when he'd asked about her wedding photographer. She'd been nervous, but she'd used her fiancé's name. That didn't seem like a lie to him.

"If her fiancé is gone as much as she says he is, she just might be lonely."

"Not our problem," Preeti said, suddenly all business.

She slid out of the booth clutching a red patent leather bag which Peter knew would have some fancy designer's name on it.

"I have to get back to work. Fashion waits for no woman." She beamed, looking as though she were trying not to.

He stood, scooped up the bill, and fished his wallet out of his back pocket. "Let me give you a lift."

"Seriously? You think I want to be dropped off in that?" She flicked her gaze to the truck. "I'll take the bus, thanks. It's only about ten minutes to the office."

"Suit yourself." He grinned at her. "See ya later, sis."

Preeti headed for the door, and he made his way to the till to pay. He only had to wait a moment for Melinda to show up to take his money.

"Say, uh," he began, not quite sure where he was going next.

She glanced up, then back down at the keys,

pecking furiously.

"Hey, my girlfriend and I are going to the movies tonight . . . you know that theatre down on Macleod Trail?"

The waitress nodded and the cash register jingled.

"Eighteen ninety-five, please."

He handed her a twenty and kept talking. "Maybe you . . . I mean, you and Robert, if he's around . . . uh, would you guys like to come on a double date with us? And if he's not, you are still welcome to come. Anise is really great. She won't mind at all."

He hoped he was right about Anise not minding. Things hadn't been going so well between them lately. Women could be funny about having other pretty women around, he'd noticed, even if they were on the arm of another guy.

And the girl looking at him with those wide grey eyes was definitely pretty, just a little . . . tired, maybe.

She cleared her throat as she handed him the change. "Thank you, but Robert is flying in this afternoon, and we already have plans for tonight. Some other time, maybe."

He nodded, pocketing his change. "Some other time."

"Myers! Order up!" yelled a chunky bald man in a folded white cap and grubby apron from the kitchen pass-through window behind her.

"Coming, Fred!" she called back, and was gone.

Peter slowly walked to the table, left a tip for her, and headed out to the parking lot.

At least he'd tried. That's all anyone could ask. Wasn't it?

Chapter 3

MELINDA FUMBLED WITH THE keys to her apartment. She seemed to have lost the ability to fit them into the lock. They rattled to the carpeted floor with a clang and she let out a growl of frustration. A second try was more successful, and she stumbled through the door.

In truth, the entire afternoon had been a bit of a blur. Whenever she hadn't kept a tight leash on her thoughts, they wandered from the task at hand to an image of dreamy's face—his perfect teeth, his wavy black hair, and his strong chin. And that dimple! Did God really make humans so perfect?

Just remembering him utter her name in his mellifluous baritone made her stare off into space again.

"Melinda . . . Melinda."

The voice changed pitch to a more familiar one, and she jumped. The mental image shifted—black hair became dark brown, and nearly black eyes transformed into piercing blue ones above the collar of a white captain's shirt. The perfect teeth didn't change, still giving her a dazzling smile that could melt her in seconds.

"See you tonight, baby," the new face said.

"Robert," she whispered.

The image faded, and she found herself staring at her own face in her hall mirror. Even in the dim light, she could see the dark circles under her eyes and the beginnings of worry lines forming around her mouth, created by the habitual grim set of her lips. She studied her own face, trying to remember a time when she looked happy. After a moment, she turned away in disgust.

As she entered the bedroom to change, Melinda ran her hand down the dress hanging from the door before putting it on. Sleeveless, with a sweetheart neckline and pleated waist, the retro design did not seem at all at odds with the modern fabric. The gauzy silk chiffon overlay added just enough mystery without taking away any of the modesty.

She wondered what Robert would think of the skulls-and-roses look. The world lurched into greyscale, and now all those skulls made her think of was death. The feeling of accomplishment faded. She zipped the dress up her own back and headed to the bathroom.

Half an hour later, she emerged, her hair curled and up, her makeup perfect, and strappy black sandals on her feet. She silently packed up a worn picnic basket with two champagne glasses, a sandwich, and some fruit. The bottle that went in was real champagne for once—Peter's tip had been much more generous than she was used to, and she had felt like splurging a little.

Why had Peter invited her out tonight?

Not just me. Robert and me.

Still, most of her customers didn't look at her twice. Well, there were always those guys that were especially rude—the kind that thought being a diner waitress meant taking catcalls, pinches, and solicitations were part of her job description, regardless of the ring on her left hand. She had developed a pretty thick skin, and a repertoire of biting comments that shut unwanted attention down fast. If that failed, Fred would roar out and send those customers packing—he had a zero-tolerance policy when it came to harassing his girls.

But Melinda wasn't used to someone expressing an interest in her. Like Peter. She wondered idly what movie he and his girlfriend were planning to see—then realized what she was doing and broke off that line of thought with an irritated, "I'm such an idiot."

She grabbed her black shrug and the picnic basket and hurried out the front door without so much as a glance at the transformed woman who passed by the hall mirror. She had dressed up for Robert, and no one else, just like she did every Friday night.

Her favourite park near the zoo was only a few blocks away on the Bow River. The sun was perched on the skyline behind her when she found her special spot, spread out the blanket and picnic items, and sat down on a hill facing the water. Poplars in full leaf whispered in the slight breeze, and a pair of Canada geese bobbed in an eddy across the creek. She watched them as she ate her sandwich, taking the occasional sip of champagne. The mating pair were often there when she came. She had named them John and Mary. Despite herself, she found a spontaneous smile on her face for the second time today.

Mary stood in the shallows and dipped her head down into the water for a tasty morsel, while John kept a wary eye out from the bank. They alternated eating and watching, making quiet conversation with each other as they browsed. A man appeared on the hill above them with a big Great Dane on a leash, startling the pair. They flapped away, scolding loudly, their wings smacking the water as they fled.

Melinda sighed and turned to her companion.

"John and Mary are still here, Robert. Did you notice? Strange how they always come back. Just like us."

She paused, chewing, then turned to the framed

five-by-seven photo propped on the blanket next to her, a flute of champagne balanced beside it. To-night, however, the blue eyes and dimpled smile in pilot's uniform seemed somewhat accusing, and she couldn't look at him for long.

Melinda ignored her own guilty thoughts by gazing at the river. She grabbed the second glass of champagne, took a sip and murmured, "How do you like my dress?"

THE next several weeks passed in pretty much the same routine as the last three years. On Saturday morning, Melinda tucked the sketch for this week's dress into her purse, and then took the bus to the fabric store on her way home from work to find fab-ric for it.

Starting Saturday evening, and continuing on through her two days off, she managed to get her dress pattern made, the fabric cut and draped on the dress form, and the garment basted together. By Tuesday night, she had made the necessary fitting ad-justments and had begun to sew permanent seams with her machine.

Her small kitchen table was the hub of all her ac-tivity—she hadn't used it for eating for years. The dress form barely fit into the space between the table and the stacks of boxes that filled her living room almost to the ceiling. There were row upon row of similar boxes, each with a sheet of loose leaf taped to the side. After her weekly picnics in the park, each dress was carefully laid in its box on top of the pattern she had used to make it, added to the pile, and barely received another thought afterwards.

As the temperatures dipped from late summer warmth into the chill of early fall, the designs included longer sleeves or a woollen cropped jacket. Silhouettes varied from slender shift-dresses to pleated or gathered knee-length skirts. But always the colours were in monochromatic greys and blacks, with the occasional splash of red or vibrant pink thrown in.

Like blood and death, Melinda had thought grimly when she noticed the trend in her colour choices. But she didn't change her selections.

And often, as she crawled between her blankets, she would say to the man in the picture frame on her bed stand, "I'm making a new dress, Robert. You're going to love it."

ONE morning, she found the napkin Peter had given her. She stared at it in dismay.

Peter Surati.

Why had she told him she'd call him? The very idea was ludicrous.

Perhaps because you turned into a blathering idiot when you talked to him, the voice in her head accused.

She crumpled the napkin and tossed it in the

trash, along with the warmth she'd felt while talking to him.

It was safer this way. For both of them.

Chapter 4

A FEW WEEKS AFTER his first appearance, the handsome Asian Indian man with the disarming smile was back in Melinda's section. Melinda blinked, her mouth going dry. She looked around for Sandra so she could give the table to her, but the other waitress was on her break.

Fred caught her eye through the pass-through window. He jabbed a finger at Peter, then pointed at the corners of his mouth, giving her a smile that looked more like a grimace to indicate his message. His meaning was clear.

She took a deep breath. She could do this. She could make Fred happy and not allow herself to swim into dangerous waters at the same time.

She pasted on a smile she knew was more nervous than welcoming, but she really was trying. She turned to Fred to show him, pointing at her own face with her eyebrows raised in question. He rolled his eyes and let out a loud puff of air. A whole horde of butterflies had invaded her abdomen, but she widened the smile a bit more and headed out on the floor.

She approached Peter's booth, sucked in a deep breath, and wiped her sweaty palms on her apron before speaking.

"Hello." Her cheeks had begun to ache. "Iced tea again?"

Peter smiled warmly. "Hi, Melinda! I was hoping I'd see you here today. Iced tea is fine. Also, I brought something for you to look at."

He patted a large brown book beside his elbow on the table that looked like it might be a photo album.

Melinda glanced around—it was a pretty slow lunch rush for a Tuesday. She might be able to take a look. But Fred had been watching her like a hawk, and he didn't like his girls sitting down with the customers, even for a few moments. A quick glance over her shoulder confirmed that he was watching her now with a furrowed brow in between prepping burgers and toasting sandwich bread.

"What is it?" she asked.

"Just some photos I have taken. Not much of a portfolio, but that's why I wanted to talk to you. I figured that if you like what you see enough, I would give you and Robert a deal on your wedding photos in exchange for helping me to accumulate some more advertising material. Or maybe engagement photos?" The hopeful, boyish grin he gave her only accentuated his handsome face.

Her heart thumped. *Careful, Melinda.*

"Robert and I already had our engagement photos done, sorry."

His grin faltered, and she softened. He was trying so hard to make this work. The least she could do was encourage him to follow his passion, even if she wouldn't be able to hire him.

"But we haven't hired a photographer yet. I would love to see it, but I can't look at it while I'm working. Uh, can you stop by after work today?"

There wouldn't be any harm in that.

He brightened once more. "Tell you what. I can't come back today, but I'll come by some other afternoon when you're off work, if that's okay. How about Thursday? Five-thirty, you said?"

Melinda nodded. "Sounds good."

She caught Peter winking roguishly at Fred as she strode off to get his drink order. Fred let out another puff of air and started ignoring her so pointedly it was almost as bad as when he was watching her. Almost. She let herself feel a bit of gratitude toward the dark-skinned man.

As Melinda served him lunch, then cleared his dishes away, Peter kept trying to engage her in conversation. When she brought him an iced tea refill, he asked about Robert. She was surprised to find herself talking about him—*really* talking about him—for the first time in years.

"We met at, uh, the sports shop. By the skis," she said, shifting her weight. "He was looking for the 'perfect pair' of downhill skis. I was looking for the bathroom. I had my head up, looking for the washroom sign, and ran into him. Literally." She grinned wryly at the memory.

"Really? Guess that worked out for the best," Peter said, chuckling. "Anise keeps trying to convince me that we should go skiing at Whistler this winter, but I'm a little nervous about it. Do you ski?"

"No. Robert kept, I mean, *keeps* promising to take me, but we, uh, never seem to have the time." Her explanation came out in a rush. "He works so much, and when he is home, he just wants to relax. Not that I blame him." She paused, embarrassed. "I don't know—I'm not a big 'outdoor winter sports' person," she mumbled.

"Growing up in Mumbai, I wasn't either, for some reason," Peter said with an overly straight face.

She was shocked to hear an actual giggle coming out of her throat. How long had it been since she had laughed?

Peter's face cracked into a grin. "Ah, so you do have a smile in there somewhere." He clasped his hands and stretched, cracking his knuckles. "My work here is done."

Melinda's eyes widened, and for a moment she wondered if the reason he seemed so interested in her was because Fred had put him up to this. She glanced at her boss, who had resumed scowling at her through the pass-through window, and pushed the thought aside. Fred would never hire someone to get her to smile—he would just fire her.

Peter started sliding out of the booth. She took a step back to get out of his way.

"I guess I better get back on the road—my work there is *never* done." Peter gave an exaggerated sigh.

She rang his order through the till and stood watching him until his cheerful "See you Thursday!" was cut off by the door jangling behind him. Then she moved to clean up his table. He was already pulling out of the parking lot when she found his generous tip covered by a napkin. *Keep smiling!* was scrawled across the paper in a loose hand.

Her gaze followed the tail lights of the cube van as they turned out of the parking lot.

A puzzled smile was on her lips.

Peter did come back Thursday, but for lunch, and without the photo album. Then Friday. And Wednesday. In fact, he suddenly became her most regular customer.

The fact did not go unnoticed. "What's with this

guy that keeps showing up to visit ya, hun?" Sandra drawled one day as Melinda poured his iced tea. "Is he sweet on you or somethin'? You planning to lead him along the cherry lane? I've always thought chocolate ice cream much more interesting than vanilla, myself." She raised her eyebrows meaningfully. "'Specially for cherry-picking." She started collecting her order from under the heat lamps.

Melinda had never quite learned how to deal with this sort of teasing. "Stop it, Sandra. He's just a nice guy who is trying to get me to hire him as our wedding photographer. Nothing more. Besides, he has a girlfriend, so why would he be hitting on me?"

"Humph, if you say so. You know, when you're not glaring at folks like you're Morticia Addams, you've actually got something going on there, sweet thang."

Sandra's overly-made-up eyes sparkled mischievously. Before Melinda could think of something—*anything*—to say in response, Sandra swept away with three plates stacked up her left arm and another in her right hand.

Melinda stood there with her mouth open. Closing it firmly, she smoothed non-existent wrinkles out of her apron to regain her composure. Then she gave her head a little shake and went to take Peter's order.

PETER made it a game to get Melinda to smile or laugh every time he visited. Rarely at a loss for a funny story, he would ramble about his girlfriend or stories about growing up in his crazy family in India, and he always succeeded in getting a warm response from Melinda—often more than once. He was pleased to note that her genuine smiles came quicker and more often with each succeeding visit.

However, despite their increasing rapport, Peter quickly learned that Melinda was not going to be forthcoming with information about her own family.

"So, Melinda, tell me about yourself. Brothers or sisters?" he asked one day as she set his drink on the table.

"No," she replied, shifting her weight.

"And your parents? Where are they?"

Melinda's forehead furrowed, and her lips became firm. "My mom died when I was little, so I don't remember much about her. My dad died a few years ago. So now it's just me."

Peter mentally kicked himself for being such a prying idiot. No wonder she didn't ever talk about her family. And good luck getting her to bring out that beatific smile now.

"I'm so sorry to hear that. It must have been so hard for you to lose your dad."

Melinda sighed. "No need to apologize. It's not like it was your fault." She poised her pen to take his order.

Peter tried to regain the ground he had lost. "At

least you have Robert, right?"

Her pinched expression was not the response he had expected.

"Yes, Robert. Of course." She smiled weakly. "What are you having for lunch today?"

He decided that the smile counted and ordered a large cheeseburger, relieved to leave the topic behind.

Peter folded his hands beneath his chin and watched her swish away. She called his order back to the kitchen and poked the chit on the little spinning wheel above the pass-through counter for the cooks, the picture of efficiency. When she glanced his way, he flashed her a grin, but she frowned and looked away.

He pressed his lips together. He supposed he deserved that for being so nosy.

He couldn't quite get a handle on this girl. She clammed up every time he asked her about herself, and after the conversation they'd just had, he had begun to understand why. He should probably take the hint and back off, but for some reason, he couldn't.

Maybe Preeti was right. Maybe there was no Robert, and Melinda was wearing that ring as a great big *leave me alone* sign. But after the stories she'd shared about Robert, he couldn't believe that. No, it had to be something else. But what?

Leave it alone, Peter. She's not your responsibility.

But he couldn't avoid the niggling sensation that it

might be. She was grieving—that much was obvious. He knew grief too well, and how important it was to have people to talk to when you were mired in it. The few glimmers of joy he'd managed to draw from between her clouds encouraged him. Maybe it wasn't his job to help her learn to live again. Then again, whose job was it? The fiancé she saw for a few days a week? What if she had no one else?

And what if Robert were a lie after all, and she wore that ring as a shield against the pain that surrounded her?

No, not that. But there was . . . something. A story he definitely wanted to know more about. Maybe he should bring Anise to meet her. As a woman, she might have more luck breaking through those barriers.

He surreptitiously watched her as she moved around the diner. He would keep befriending her. Oh, he'd be careful—he had Anise and Robert to think about. But he wouldn't simply walk away, not unless she made it plain that she wanted him to.

He didn't even think he could.

Chapter 5

MELINDA ROLLED THE CIRCULAR blade of the rotary cutter along the edge of the pattern piece, neatly duplicating its shape in the fabric laid out carefully below. The kitchen table was not really big enough for cutting out most skirts, so she usually used the floor of her small galley-style kitchen. Despite the ache in her back, her mind wandered as she fell into the hypnotic rhythm of the process— trace the edge of a pattern piece with the razor-sharp blade, move the large, green mat which protected the linoleum to a new position below the fabric, repeat.

Making dresses was so simple. She loved the feel of the fabric and deciding whether this one or that one had better drape for the project she had in mind. She loved taking a flat piece of cloth and making it into a beautiful item of clothing. She loved how subtle changes in the way a pattern was cut could drastically affect the final garment's shape. She loved how she knew exactly what to do to create a dress— you did step A, then step B, and so on until you were finished. And even if you made a mistake, it was very seldom unfixable with a little extra time and effort.

Not like life. Not like life at all.

As she cut, she heard her mother's voice, and her own chubby six-year-old hands seemed superimposed over the adult ones in front of her.

Lay the pattern straight on the grain of the fabric or it won't hang right. Be careful, Melly, you don't want to cut yourself.

They had made a little skirt for her to wear to school, red gingham with a black felt appliquéd poodle on it. She had loved working on that project with her mother, loved knowing that they had made something beautiful together.

Melinda remembered the first time she wore that skirt. All day, the feeling of wearing something she had made herself buoyed up her spirits in a way she had never experienced before. Her best friend had been completely amazed, and Melinda glowed in the admiration she could see in her friend's eyes. For the first time in her life, she'd felt special.

Her insides were still effervescent on the bus ride home from school. It was while the bus was waiting at the stop light to turn toward the subdivision where she lived that the unthinkable happened.

Melinda was sitting on the right side of the bus by the window. Looking absently through the glass, she spotted her mother's car waiting to cross the intersection and waved excitedly. Her mother spied her and waved back, smiling, before the light changed and the car slowly started accelerating.

That was the last time she saw her mother alive.

The pickup that ran the red light exploded onto the scene like a bomb. The next few seconds were a cacophony of images and sounds that haunted Melinda in slow-motion nightmares for years to come—the blur of red and chrome, the ear-splitting squeal, the acrid stench of rubber sliding on asphalt, the jagged rending of crushing metal, the shattering glass spraying all over the pavement, her mother's green station wagon crumpled like a deflated accordion. She didn't even realize she had been screaming until she stopped to draw in a ragged breath.

Melinda had told her father that she hadn't seen her mother in the car after the accident, and he had been visibly relieved.

But she lied.

She *wished* she hadn't, and she thought by denying it she could forget the sight of her mother's broken body and lifeless eyes staring upward as her lifeblood seeped onto the vinyl seats.

Had her mother not been waving to her, would she have seen the truck speeding toward her? The thought reverberated inside Melinda's head for the millionth time with the same gut-twisting ache. Some questions had no answers.

The cutter slipped off the edge of the mat, and she cursed aloud. A close inspection of the linoleum revealed no harm done, and she breathed a sigh of relief, which turned into a grunt of disgust when she noticed that she had nicked the fabric inside the edge of her pattern piece. After a few moments' examination, she decided she could work around it in the design, adjusted her mat, and continued cutting.

Peter had been in the diner again yesterday, but he hadn't come alone this time. He had cheerfully introduced her to his girlfriend, but Melinda's polite comment about having heard so many good things about the woman backfired. Melinda froze in mid-sentence when she sensed the sub-zero chill coming off of the ginger-haired, freckled beauty.

There had been no friendly banter about Robert, Preeti, or anything else that lunch hour. Melinda had done only what was necessary to serve their table, and the few snippets of conversation she caught as she came and went were sharp-edged and terse. Finally, Anise swept out of the diner, leaving her soup and salad unfinished, and Peter pushed his burger and fries away from him, half-eaten.

As Melinda came by to collect the plates, Peter had given her a weak smile.

"Thanks, Melinda," he said, then gazed out the window with unfocused eyes.

Melinda kept glancing at him worriedly as she rang up his bill.

She cautiously approached him. "Hey, are you okay?" She laid the slip in front of him.

He glanced at her, but he still looked dazed.

"No, not really, I guess . . . but I know I will be. Don't know when, but it will happen." He gave a snort of derision and looked down. "Anise just broke up with me." He exhaled loudly and shifted in his seat. "Okay, actually, no. I broke up with her, after she admitted to me that she had cheated on me." He looked back out the window. "Again."

Melinda slowly sank onto the bench seat across from him. "I'm . . . I'm so sorry, Peter."

"Well, you'd think by now, I wouldn't be so surprised," he muttered.

Melinda waited, not quite sure what he meant.

"Why do I have such stellar taste in women?" he said with a mocking laugh.

Melinda studied Peter's face, not prompting him, but not urging him along with her body language, either. He needed someone to listen. He would speak when he was ready.

"Well, I guess that's not important to you. We barely know each other. I'm sorry, Melinda, I shouldn't be dumping this all on you. I'm sure you have enough problems of your own to deal with."

"What do you mean by that?" she asked, a little startled.

Peter's eyes widened slightly. "Oh, uh, nothing. I mean, we all have our own problems, don't we? Mine is just choosing the wrong kind of women. Maybe I'll give up dating altogether." He stared grimly at the tabletop, which was the same robin's egg-blue as Melinda's diner uniform.

"Peter," Melinda said gently, "Not all women are like Anise. There are plenty of decent and loving girls out there looking for a wonderful guy like you. You're fun, you're caring, you're handsome . . . you have so much going for you. You just haven't found that special girl who will be The One for you yet. That's all."

Peter looked at her, his eyes murky black pools of sadness. She felt like she was drowning in them.

Then his eyebrows lifted, and his gaze softened. "Well, Melly—I mean, Melinda, if you see all that in me, I guess I won't give up yet. That Robert must be one amazing guy to have kept a girl like you. Lucky, too."

He always rolled his R's slightly, so *girl* sounded a bit like a shortened *gull*. Melinda enjoyed listening to him speak so much it took her a moment to realize what he had just said. When she did, she sat up straight, and she heard her father's voice muttering something about *the tangled webs we weave*. How dare she be thinking about drowning in his eyes! She would have to be more careful.

He saw her expression and tensed. "Did I say something wrong?"

"My mother used to call me 'Melly'." Her hands were suddenly busy smoothing her apron and tightening her pony tail, eyes looking anywhere but at his.

"Oh, I'm sorry," said Peter hurriedly. "I won't call you that again, if you don't want me to."

Sandra swept by with an armful of dirty dishes.

"Melinda, Fred's giving you the evil eye," she stage-whispered.

A quick glance over Melinda's shoulder confirmed Sandra's words, and she jumped to her feet.

Peter was already fishing in his wallet for a few bills. "Keep the change," he said grimly, sliding out of the booth.

Melinda thanked him and pocketed the cash, reluctantly turning to get back to work. She hesitated, then swivelled back and lightly touched his arm. He stopped near enough that she could feel the heat from his body.

"You can call me Melly if you want to, Peter."

There were those eyes again, and in such close proximity! She dropped her arm and took a step back, a little breathless.

"And . . . please feel free to talk to me any time," she got out. "About anything."

Peter nodded, and she hurried away, chased by a loud snort from Fred.

WITH the last fabric piece finally cut, Melinda stood and stretched her aching back, then cleaned up the mess on the floor.

Why had she told Peter that? *Idiot!*

But it had been so nice to have someone talk to her—notice her——the way Peter had been doing lately, and then to confide in her, like a friend. How long since someone had done that? And how long since she had had someone to talk to that didn't stare back frozenly from behind a framed piece of glass?

You would have *someone to talk to if you didn't push everyone away*, the voice in her head accused. But she knew she had good reason for that.

As if presenting an indictment, the phone rang. Melinda glanced at the number and let it continue ringing. Eventually, the answering machine kicked on, and her own voice echoed as if from the bottom of a well.

"This is Melinda. Leave a message."

After the high-pitched squeal, Robert's sister came on the line. Her voice reflected the forced cheer of repeatedly talking to a machine instead of the actual person.

"Hey, Melinda, it's Nadia. Mom and I are coming to the city in a couple of days to go shopping, and we were wondering if we could meet up with you for lunch or something. We could come by the diner, if it would work better for you. Call me back and let me know. You know the number." She paused. "It would be great to see you, Mel. It's been way too long." Another pause. "Okay, well. Call me."

The phone clicked, and the machine squealed again.

Melinda ignored it, like she always did, and started pinning the bodice of her dress together on the dress form. Glancing at the photo in the rustic wooden frame on her kitchen cabinet, she jumped a little and pricked her thumb. Muttering to herself, she sucked on the droplet of blood that appeared and examined the spot. No more red seeped out, and she breathed a sigh of relief—blood was so tricky to get out of wool, and she didn't want to have to stop working for longer than necessary.

Guiltily, she peeked at the engagement photo again. Robert's brightly smiling face looked back at her, arm around a girl that could have been Melinda's younger, happier, more carefree twin sister. The couple in the photo looked so happy together.

For a moment—just a fraction of a second—she could have sworn that the man in the photo had been Peter.

She shook her head and went back to work.

Chapter 6

MELINDA SIPPED HER TEA, then returned the white stoneware mug to its saucer on the linen tablecloth and turned the page, her eyes riveted to the unfolding story of Moll Flanders. She was lounging in the upscale Ambrosia, a restaurant in the five-star L'Hotêl LaValle—just a patron having a solitary supper before heading out for a party in her charcoal grey dupioni silk dress. At least, she hoped she appeared that way.

The slightly slubbed fabric of this Friday's dress had a wonderful sheen that was the perfect match for the slim, sheath-like silhouette of the design. A pleated drape began at the side seam of her right underarm, then crossed the bodice at a diagonal and was fixed in place over her left shoulder by a black-stained wooden spiral button before falling in neat folds behind her to the knee-length hem of the skirt.

The look faintly echoed an Indian-style sari—one of her more clever fashion adaptations.

Peter strode across the hotel lobby, camera dangling on his chest. He glanced through the decorative window panes of the hotel restaurant on his way by and stopped short. It took only a stuttering heartbeat to recognize the enchanting woman sitting by herself on the other side of the glass. Melinda's dark hair was piled on top of her head, and her pendant earrings swung alluringly like miniature pendulums against her cheek. She was so engrossed in an antique hardcover, she didn't notice him pause to regard her.

The room suddenly seemed a bit too warm. Melinda was absolutely stunning. But why was she sitting there all dressed up and alone? He entered the restaurant and approached her table. She didn't look up.

"Melinda?"

She glanced at him with a small start, but alarm quickly transformed into a smile.

His stomach gurgled, but he ignored it. "I hardly recognized you. You look amazing!"

She fidgeted with the edges of the pages. Her smile faded.

"Peter. What are you doing here?" she asked evenly.

"Preeti hired me to cover a big shindig that *Fresh* is putting on in the ballroom," he said, lifting the camera by way of explanation. "I was just on my way back from the washroom when I saw you. And you? You're pretty dressed up for a date with Mr. Dafoe," he grinned, indicating the battered novel that she still held.

MELINDA closed the book and placed it on the table, her face hot. She hated lying to him, but there was no way she was going to tell the truth. The lie was all she had left of Robert. The lie was the only thing protecting Peter.

Protecting herself.

"Robert's flight home was cancelled at the last minute, so he couldn't be here for our date tonight. Since I was already all dressed up, I thought I would at least go out for tea. I like this restaurant. It's quiet." *And I don't usually see anyone I know.*

"Oh. I'm sorry to hear that Robert couldn't make it. Having tea in a fancy restaurant does seem like the sensible thing to do in that situation."

He grinned crookedly, and Melinda found herself smiling involuntarily. The same way that puppies and babies always made her smile.

"Hey, do you think Robert would mind if I invited you to hang out with me at the *Fresh* party? It would be nice to have someone I know to talk to. I'll have to take some photos throughout the evening, but other than that, we are free to mock the muck-a-mucks and divas of either gender as much as we want." He gave her another boyish grin, his eyes dancing.

"Um . . ." Melinda twisted her ring, warring with herself.

The thought of a party with lots of people she didn't know, not to mention spending the whole evening with a man she only knew from work made her utterly uncomfortable. But on the other hand, there was a fiercely lonely part of her soul that was hungry—no, *ravenous*—for genuine human interaction. If she went home now, she would spend the rest of the night wallowing in regrets.

"No, I don't think he would mind."

"Really?" Peter let out a breath. "Great!"

The relief on his face nearly made her change her mind—but what harm could there be in going to a party? He'd be working the whole time, anyway. And she could leave whenever she wanted.

She downed the dregs from her cup before standing and gathering her wrap and purse, and then left a few dollars for the tea and a tip on the table.

"After you, m'lady." He gestured toward the arched restaurant entrance with a flourish.

Melinda gave him a reserved smile in return as she swept past. Her four-inch heels almost let her look him in the eye.

What are you doing? said the familiar voice of doubt.

She promptly squelched any misgivings. *Just having a bit of fun.*

In the ballroom, everything seemed glittery—the patrons in a stunning array of formal wear, the fabulous decorations on the tightly-packed round tables, the disco ball hanging over the hardwood dance floor. Even the stage was adorned with glittering silver garlands and floral arrangements. Melinda ran her hands down the muted grey silk of her dress self-consciously.

"Peter!" She tugged on his sleeve and yelled in his ear to be heard over the loud techno-dance music emanating from the speakers set up by the stage. "I don't think I quite fit in here."

He raised his eyebrows. "Are you kidding?" he exclaimed. "You look perfectly enchanting. Like Audrey Hepburn crossed with Madhubala."

He gave her the once-over approvingly.

She nodded uncertainly, confused by the unfamiliar reference, and continued to follow him. He looked casually stunning in black dress pants, an eggplant-coloured button-down shirt with the sleeves rolled up almost to his elbows, and a striped tie, no jacket.

A woman in an exquisite sequined floor-length backless red dress strolled by on the arm of a man in a black tuxedo. The woman's glance took Melinda in within a single instant—approvingly—before she moved past. Melinda relaxed a little. Maybe Peter was right.

And had he actually compared her with Audrey Hepburn? She blushed in delayed embarrassment at the compliment, glad that he couldn't see her face as she tailed him along the edge of the crowded room.

PETER found Melinda a place to sit near the back wall, away from all the high-traffic areas, and got her a cocktail to sip—virgin, at her request. He returned to her table frequently after roaming to various locations to capture the evening's highlights.

Dinner was already over, and people were milling around as servers cleared dessert dishes and refreshed coffee. The table was empty except for a middle-aged woman wearing a sparkling black sheath dress. She had a chin-length black bob with a streak of silver on one side framing a handsome but classically made-up face. The woman smiled at Melinda, then took a sip of garnet-hued wine while she looked her over. Melinda was relieved the loud music made pleasantries next to impossible, even from just across a banquet table. She smiled politely at the woman, then turned away to watch the room at large.

"Who are you wearing?" came a throaty woman's voice with a mild French accent.

Melinda started. The woman had moved around the table to sit next to her. She indicated Melinda's dress.

"Who are you wearing?" she repeated. "It's stunning."

Melinda's throat felt thick. "Oh, uh, this is just something I made."

The woman's eyes widened almost imperceptibly. "And you are?"

Melinda's face warmed. "Oh, I'm no one. Just a friend of the photographer's." She smiled and stood, avoiding the woman's bemused gaze. "Excuse me, I have to go find him."

She stood and edged along the back of the room until she spotted Peter approaching her. She caught his eye and made her way toward him, and had almost reached him when she was hailed by a familiar voice.

"Peter! There you are!" exclaimed a woman in an open-R'd accent that Melinda immediately recognized as Preeti.

Melinda stopped a few paces away, trying to melt into the wall, and gaped at the gorgeous, perfectly-coiffed diminutive Indian woman whose sequined stilettos were clicking purposefully toward them. Caught in Preeti's wake was a slim brunette that looked like she should be in a grey pencil skirt and holding a clipboard, not the floor-length forest-green gown she currently wore. She was even more businesslike than her boss.

"Oh, heya, Preeti." Peter lowered his camera to look at her. "Time for the show to start?"

"Yes, soon. I just want to make sure you take photos of a few specific people. Bonnie, please give him the list."

Preeti's shadow handed over an unsealed envelope. Peter took it, looking slightly incredulous.

"And how, dear sister, am I to know who these people are by only a name?"

Preeti gave an exaggerated sigh that made her glittering diamond earrings swing. "There are descriptions, too."

Peter pulled out the paper and quickly scanned the contents.

"There have to be close to a hundred names here. Do you want me to memorize descriptions or take pictures?" He snorted in amusement. "I know. How about I make sure to take photos of all the well dressed people, okay? I'm sure that should about cover it."

Preeti glared her response. "Just don't miss any of them, alright?"

With a glare at Peter that echoed Preeti's, Bonnie touched her employer's arm. "Time for the speeches, Preeti. You need to go."

"Right, thank you." Preeti took a step and stopped. "Well, Peter? Are you coming?"

"Of course. I'm right behind you," Peter replied, a hint of exasperation creeping into his voice.

Preeti gave a satisfied nod and clicked away, Bonnie only a step behind.

Peter tucked the folded list into his shirt pocket and turned to Melinda apologetically.

"I'll be back soon."

He gave Melinda's arm a quick squeeze and strode off to a vantage point near the stage.

Melinda found a nearby empty seat and settled herself down to listen to the speakers as, onstage, a woman in a floor-length black gown introduced Preeti. Vivacious and stunning, Preeti swept forward to the podium and took control of the room. Her short speech about the re-launch of "Western Canada's hottest women's interest magazine" and their focus on the modern woman—a woman who was timeless, edgy, and fresh—was met with resounding applause.

Melinda couldn't help marvel at Preeti's poise. She couldn't imagine speaking to a room of fifteen, let alone two hundred fifty. But Preeti didn't even break a sweat.

After the applause faded, Preeti welcomed many of the guests specifically by name before introducing the keynote speaker, Madame Bouvier, an instructor from one of Canada's foremost design colleges in Toronto.

Madame Bouvier! Melinda turned, wondering what a fashion icon would look like, and nearly fell off her chair when the woman who had been sharing a table with her earlier ascended the steps to the stage. The woman adjusted the podium mic up to her height and turned to face the crowd, her dark eyes sparkling with vitality.

"Fashion. It's more than the clothes we wear," Madame Bouvier began, her gaze roving around the room. She looked in Melinda's direction, and though she couldn't possibly see her past the blinding spotlight, Melinda's breath caught. "It is the story we tell the world about ourselves. Our clothes reveal who we are and how we relate to the world—and how we want the world to relate to us."

Melinda swallowed and her palms grew slick.

I was talking to Madame Bouvier.

"For designers," Madame Bouvier continued, "this is even more true. Every time we create a new design, not only do we create a piece of art, we are telling the world who we are. But whether you are a designer or not, you are someone with a story to tell—and someone out there needs to hear your words. And that means none of us, not a single person in this room, is no one. You have only to accept that the world needs to hear what you have to say."

Melinda thought of what she'd said to Madame Bouvier when she'd asked who Melinda was and blushed. Was Madame Bouvier talking to her? But who would want to hear her story—the girl from nowhere with nothing to recommend her? The educator continued, but Melinda barely heard her words. How could someone so accomplished find merit in her work? She shook her head. Maybe Madame Bouvier had just been being polite.She took a deep breath and made herself focus on the woman's words, soaking up every drop of knowledge she could catch in a twenty-minute speech. She might not fit in with the famous and up-and-coming designers in the room, but she didn't want to waste this opportunity to learn from one of the foremost fashion professionals in the country. Every sentence the woman uttered seemed utterly profound. By the time Madame Bouvier left the stage, Melinda's head was spinning, but her heart rate had almost slowed down to normal.

Until she remembered that meant Peter would be coming for her again soon. She could see him on the far side of the stage, picking his way toward her through the crowd that was flooding onto the dance floor. He had almost reached her when Preeti caught up to him again.

"How's it going so far, Peter?"

Peter shook his head at her, looking both amused and annoyed. "Just fine. You really need to relax, sis."

He put his hand on Preeti's elbow and guided her over to Melinda. Melinda politely stood to greet her.

"You remember Melinda, right? I found her sitting

in the hotel restaurant, and since her date couldn't meet her, I insisted she come hang out with me." Peter winked at Melinda as if they shared a private joke, his smile mischievous.

Preeti looked confused for a moment, then recognition and a practised smile blanketed her face. She offered Melinda her hand.

"Of course. From the diner, right?"

Melinda shook her head. "Yes, that's right."

Preeti's gaze swept over Melinda's outfit. "Wow, what a fabulous dress! Where did you get it?"

A pace away, Bonnie listened attentively, looking as though she were poised to take notes in her head. Peter watched the exchange with a bemused smile.

Melinda swallowed and hesitated. She didn't want a repeat of the situation with Madame Bouvier, but what could she say that wasn't an outright lie?

I've lied enough for one night. She cast a glance at Peter, her stomach twisting, then back at his sister, who still waited for an answer.

"Uh, thank you. I, uh, I had it made for me," Melinda stammered.

"Really? It is stunning work." Preeti examined the dress with an appreciative eye. "Made by whom? Anyone here?" She indicated the room.

"Just a friend who sews." Time to change the topic. "This is a wonderful party. Peter said you were the driving force behind it. You must be proud of how it all turned out."

Preeti looked pleased. "Thank you. Yes, it all turned out quite well, thankfully." Her look became distracted, and she turned back to her brother. "Peter, that reminds me. Did you get a photograph of the mayor and his wife? They look like they are getting ready to leave."

"Yes, *didi*. I am pretty sure I have shot everyone in the room twice, and all the pretty girls at least double that," he teased.

Preeti glared at him, her sense of humour a little frayed at the moment.

"A simple 'yes' would have sufficed," she snapped. "And it's my job to make sure everyone else is doing theirs."

"Never fear, Preeti." He patted her arm. "You will have plenty of photos to choose from for your press release and yearbook memories. Smile!"

He raised the camera and aimed it at her. She put on her practised smile before his camera flashed, gave him an exasperated look as he lowered it, and then spun on her stilettos and clicked away to check on something or someone else. Her assistant hurried to catch up to her employer, who was already issuing instructions over her shoulder.

"Sisters." Peter shrugged at Melinda, a rueful grin on his face. "Gotta love 'em."

"You're lucky to have one with whom you are so

close," Melinda replied wistfully.

"Well, she's okay most of the time," Peter said, glancing after his sister. "But sometimes she is a real pain in the backside."

Melinda laughed politely and shifted on her feet, the high heels pinching her toes. Her choice of footwear hadn't seemed so bad when her plans for the evening involved more sitting than standing, but she had spent most of the last couple of hours trying to stay out of the way of legitimate guests—not an easy feat in such a crowded space. On the dance floor, "The Macarena" was just getting started, and the throbbing beat pulsed in sync with the throbbing in her arches.

Some of the pain must have shown on her face, because Peter leaned in once more and said, "I'm pretty much done. You wanna get out of here? Go get some air?"

Melinda had been trying not to show how overwhelmed she was by the loud music, glittering lights, and crowds of people, but Peter seemed to notice anyway. She gave him a grateful smile and nodded.

"Just give me a minute," he said, then strode after Preeti.

Melinda sat down again and watched from a distance as the siblings had a quick exchange. She should go home. That would be the smart thing to do. But she couldn't quite make herself get up and leave.

Then Preeti nodded and Peter returned to her, tickling her ear with his warm breath.

"Okay, we're good to go."

Her stomach lurched. That was what she was afraid of.

Chapter 7

Peter and Melinda strolled through an indoor jungle in the hotel's atrium. Melinda's senses were on high alert. Hiding in the dark at the edge of the crowded ballroom, it had been easy to forget that she was there on the behest of the handsome photographer. Now that they were alone, she was aware of Peter's every move.

He strolled with his camera bag slung over his shoulder, his hands in his pockets, and an easy gait. She held her book and small black satin clutch clasped in front of her and took mincing steps, partly because of her aching feet, and partly because she couldn't seem to relax. She wanted to be here with Peter. But she knew she was inching onto some thin emotional ice.

He asked her some innocuous questions as they walked, things about the weather and what part of town she lived in, comments about the local pizza joint in her neighbourhood, and self-effacing wisecracks about his own. She chuckled despite herself, ignoring the guilty twinge in her gut. It was difficult not to laugh around Peter. He had a way about him that put her at ease despite herself.

Before long, they found themselves in the semi-privacy of a little decorative pool area. Melinda gratefully sank onto a wood-slat bench and kept her book and her clutch on her lap as she took in their surroundings. A sheet of water streamed down the surface of an elegant glass elevator shaft that descended from the high, vaulted ceiling into the wishing pond before them. It was a perfect little oasis of privacy on the edge of the busy atrium where the hotel's swimming pool was located.

Peter pulled his camera from the bag and snapped some photos of the beautiful surroundings. She surreptitiously kicked off her shoes. Her toes wiggled in delight to be free from their constraints.

Strolling in four-inch heels after a full day on your feet waitressing is now officially on my 'do not repeat' list. Right below using rubber bands for ponytail holders and slightly above eating hospital cafeteria food.

She closed her eyes, remembering the last time she'd had to do both those things while caught in a whirlwind of sleepless nights as her father slipped away from her. She bit her lip, then looked at her companion, who stood a few feet away by the edge of the pool with an expectant expression. She realized she hadn't even heard his question.

"I'm sorry, Peter, I was thinking about something else. What did you say?"

"Not a problem."

A fleeting expression of concern crossed his brow. He put his camera bag on the floor beside her and glanced down at her wiggling piggies in amusement. His camera was still slung around his neck, and he steadied it with one hand.

"I was just saying that Robert seems to be away a lot. No wonder you haven't gotten back to me about your wedding photos."

He pulled a penny from his pocket and tossed it into the pool, then watched the ripples move lazily across the surface. The sheet of water flowing down the elevator shaft created less of a disturbance sliding into the pool at the back of the pond than the coin.

"Well, you were supposed to bring your photo album back, but I never saw it again," she chided. "How am I supposed to know if you are any good?" She couldn't hold back a small smile.

"Yeah, sorry about that." He looked embarrassed. "I keep forgetting to bring it with me to work, and I can't leave it in the truck. I'll bring it to show you soon, I promise."

Melinda fidgeted with the strap of her clutch.

"How are things going in the move toward 'professional photographer,' anyway?"

"Well, I'm getting paid tonight." He gave a half-smile and tilted the camera in his hand. "It's a start, anyway."

The mischief faded from his face and his gaze dropped to her discarded shoes.

"Honestly, I really need to get my portfolio together, because I'm never going to get steady work as a photographer if I can't show people professional work I've done."

"You seem to love doing it," she said. "What got you interested in photography?"

"My sister."

He threw another penny at the pool. It looked like he was aiming for the exact spot he had thrown the last one, and when it hit the surface with a small plop short of his target, he looked annoyed. Crouching by the edge of the shallow water, he scooped out a handful of coins tossed by Wishers Past, shook the extra water from his hand, and started tossing them back in one at a time.

With him half-turned away from her, Melinda examined his profile. She wanted to drink him in, drink in his company. She had really been lonely for far too long. A blood-red alarm started flashing somewhere in the back of her mind.

She ignored it.

"Preeti? How?"

He glanced at her, then back at his next target. "No, not Preeti. My twin sister, Kanti."

Another coin landed with a plop.

"She always used to fish old magazines out of the bin to look at the pictures. We children didn't have a real camera. Papa didn't want to pay for developing the film because it was so expensive, and this was before digital cameras came out. So whenever she found a picture she really liked, she would cut it out and paste it into her scrapbook. Then she would use her fingers to pretend she was taking a picture of it. 'Click, gotcha' she would say, and laugh, framing the photo with her thumb and forefinger on each hand like this."

Peter demonstrated, creating a miniature frame with his fingers, holding it up to look at Melinda with one eye squinting as if sighting a camera, then grinned as she blushed. She found his grin to be infectious.

"Pretty soon, we would do that wherever we went. If we saw something we thought was beautiful, or striking, or silly, or whatever, we would hold up our finger-frames and say 'Click! Gotcha!'"

Melinda found herself smiling along with Peter at the memory. She set her book and clutch on the bench next to her and crossed her legs. "You've never mentioned Kanti before. Does she still live in India?"

"No." There was no hint of mischief in his voice now. "She died when we were twelve. Malaria."

"Oh," said Melinda quietly. "I'm sorry. It sounds like you two were very close."

The part of her heart that had been scarred by loss after loss contracted, pinching until her eyes started to well up. She brushed away a tear, hoping Peter hadn't seen.

"We were. She was probably my best friend, though I would never have admitted it to her. I think she knew, though." He tossed another coin.

When he glanced back at her, Melinda silently encouraged him to continue with a nod of her head.

"Before she died, I was sitting by her bed in our room. She looked so bad, you know? The doctor was just leaving, and my mother and father were speaking quietly to him by the door. Nobody would tell us kids how bad it was, but we knew it was serious." Peter's voice sounded distant with the recollection. "Kanti touched my hand and asked, 'Peter, do you think I'm pretty?'"

Peter paused for a moment, and when he spoke again, there was a catch in his voice. He tossed more coins, eyes fixed on the colliding ripples. "I didn't know what to say. At twelve, you don't know how to tell your sister that you love her more than anyone else in the world. Just like she didn't know how to ask me . . . so I just held up my finger frames and said,

'Click! Gotcha!'"

He looked down at his hands, fiddling with the few remaining coins he held.

"She smiled at me, then laid her head back and was gone, just like that."

Peter sighed and locked eyes with Melinda. She thought the lump in her throat might choke her.

"I still remember every detail of that picture of her, even though the camera was only in here." He tapped his temple. "She looked terrible, but she was so beautiful." He turned back to the pond to throw in another coin, then paused. "You know, I've never told anyone that before."

Melinda sniffed, and Peter looked at her, surprised.

"What's wrong?"

He dropped all the coins in the pond and came over to sit beside her on the bench. He moved her things aside so he could rest his hand lightly on her shoulder. She picked them up and fished for a tissue from her handbag to hide her tears.

"You'll think I'm silly." She dabbed at her eyes and sniffed again, the leak plugged for now. "Just . . . I'm sorry for your loss."

"It's alright, Melly," Peter said, reassuring her with a comforting smile. "Kanti loved life more than anyone I've ever known. I miss her terribly, even now, but I can't stop living because she did. She would not want that of me. In fact, she would probably come back from the grave to scold me soundly for even thinking of such a thing." He shook his head.

Melinda nodded, but inside of her, a dam threatened to burst. She desperately applied some emotional cement and grasped at a subject change.

"About your portfolio . . ." She took deep, controlled breaths and kept her focus on the waterfall.

"Yeah?"

She'd started. She'd have to answer now.

"I have some special dresses that I have worn on dates with Robert. If it would help, I mean, if you wanted to, you could do a photo shoot of me in some of the dresses. As long as you let me have some prints for Robert—I think it would make a very lovely gift for him."

The sudden clack of a shutter release made her glance back at Peter, who was lowering his camera.

"What was that for?"

"You looked so pretty just then, I had to take a picture." He laughed. "Click! Gotcha!"

Melinda smiled weakly.

"Don't worry, I'll give you a copy of that one for Robert, too. And I would love to do a photo shoot of you in all your pretty dresses."

He grinned, looking more boyish than ever. Melinda felt the urge to reach out and tousle his hair, but she kept her hands firmly on the purse and book in her lap.

They bantered about lighter topics, wandering around again, until Melinda said she needed to go home. Peter drove her and then walked her to the door of her apartment building.

She was just about to say goodbye when he surprised her with a kiss on her hand.

"Thank you for making my night so delightful," he said. His fingers were warm and strong around hers.

"I . . . it was so nice of you to invite me—thank you." Her face grew warm and she hurried into the building.

After her front door finally clicked closed behind her, Melinda collapsed against it with a sigh, looking guiltily at the wall of dress boxes in her living room. Peter had insisted on driving her home, and she had not tried very hard to dissuade him. Now she berated herself for agreeing to spend the evening with him at all. And for how much she enjoyed it.

And now we're going to do a photo shoot, too? She banged the back of her head gently against the door.

"What am I doing?" she moaned.

Robert stared at her accusingly from the dining room. She couldn't meet his eye.

Chapter 8

Peter fidgeted with his jeans, seated uncomfortably in a minimalist designer chair in front of a sizable glass desk in the fashion editor's office of *Fresh* magazine. The contents of the desk seemed to hang in thin air, suspended by an invisible force field. Around him, wide open spaces of white and orange and brushed stainless steel looked like they came directly from an IKEA catalogue.

It made his skin crawl.

Preeti murmured to herself as she flipped through the cardstock pages of an oversized photo album on the desk in front of her. Images of Melinda in various poses, dresses, and settings covered still other images as Preeti turned pages, sometimes nodding, and occasionally pursing her lips in thought.

"Is this in the public library?"

She indicated a photo where Melinda was poised

on a library ladder, feigning to shelve a cloth-bound hardcover copy of *Jane Eyre*. She had several other books awaiting their turn for the "librarian's" duties clasped against her light grey wool belted jumper. The knee-length sheath dress was far from demure. It had a close-fitting, narrow-waisted underbust bodice with black lace panels inset into the sides to give the illusion of an even smaller waistline and a black lace ruffle at the hem. She'd layered it over a filmy black blouse with a scoop neck and long sleeves trimmed with lace. A pair of dark-rimmed glasses borrowed from the actual librarian had completed the look.

Peter didn't have to look at the photo again for his mind's eye to see Melinda's grey ones peering over the rim of the glasses directly into his own, lips slightly parted as if inviting a kiss, just as he had captured her on the day of the shoot. Thinking of those lips, his thoughts started wandering in a direction he couldn't afford to go, and he jerked back to the present to answer Preeti's query.

"Yes. I have a friend that works there, and he let us shoot in the stacks for about an hour one afternoon. The light was perfect at that time of day. I love the whole Gothic feel of the place, too."

"Very creative how you used the intellectual setting to showcase such an alluring design, showing a woman with beauty and brains. I also love the ones you did at the laundromat—I confess, I never would have thought of that location. But it totally works."

Preeti paused and angled the book to get a better look at one particular photo, then turned the book toward him. "Where was this taken?"

It was the shot of Melinda in the grey silk dress he had snapped at L'Hotêl LaValle's terrarium, which he explained to her. Personally, it was his favourite photo of them all—the look on Melinda's face was so open and vulnerable. It was a look he had never caught there at any other time.

Preeti merely turned the album back toward her, lifting the top edge to get a better view, and studied the photo again. With a thunk, she laid the album on her desk.

"That's it, she's hired."

"*She's* hired?" Peter spluttered. "For what? I thought this was about *me* getting hired?"

"Oh, nonsense. I always knew I was going to hire you. I just wanted to see you take some initiative in the process."

Peter wasn't sure whether to be more flabbergasted or outraged. His big sister had always been a bit bossy, but really!

Preeti continued as if his jaw weren't hanging open in a rare moment of speechlessness.

"But this girl . . . I can admit when I am wrong, and this is one of those times. She has quite a striking quality to her I didn't see at first. And these dresses!"

She flipped back through the album again as she spoke, still trying to catch details she had missed.

"I absolutely *must* know who this designer friend of hers is. These designs are exactly the type of 'timeless, edgy, and fresh' look that we are going for. I want to do a complete spread with her in these, and feature her designer friend."

Preeti was on a roll, and didn't notice Peter trying to get a word in edgewise.

"Just think, a designer of this calibre living right here in Calgary. This could be a cover story! What is it, Peter? Stop stuttering like an orangutan and spit it out."

Peter gave her a look that could have frozen lava, but he took the opportunity to speak. "That's just it. I think the designer is *her*."

"What?" Preeti looked up sharply.

Peter outlined the observations he had made when he had helped Melinda carry her things right into the apartment after the photo shoot day, Melinda protesting all the while. The stacks of boxes with sketched designs tacked on them, the sewing machine and paper patterns in the dining area, and the dress form with a partially-finished gown in red and black silk all led him to believe that, as much as she denied it, the designs were all made by her, start-to-finish.

He didn't mention that he had also noticed the

framed engagement photo with the smiling couple or the dusty wedding invitation sitting on the counter for a wedding that supposedly occurred between Melinda Myers and Robert Clarkson nearly three years ago. That part of the puzzle he was still chewing on. At least he now knew Robert was a real person.

His words only fueled Preeti's fire. "This could be big. Really big. 'Diner waitress turns model and designer.' Everyone loves a good Cinderella story. She could become iconic! Give my assistant her phone number so we can get her in here right away."

Peter held up his hands as though to protect himself from the onslaught. "Preeti, slow down. I'm not so sure she is going to want to have her photos and dresses featured in your magazine. She won't even take credit for making them, for crying out loud! If you come at her with guns blazing and the spotlight already on, she'll run so fast you won't even see the *shadow* of the dust."

That took the wind out of Preeti's sails a bit. She chewed her lower lip and clicked her nails on the glass desktop. Peter recognized that look—it was the one she had when she was determined to get her way. She was not going to let this go.

Preeti met his gaze, the unspoken request in her eyes backed by determination as hard as steel.

"Oh, no." He waved his hands. "She was already doing me a favour just by letting me take these." He pointed at the album.

"If I recall, she's done a few favours for you already—coming to the party, doing the photo shoot. What's one more?" She batted her lashes at him.

No wonder she got this job. He could feel himself yielding before that will as strong as a hurricane.

Finally, he sighed. "Fine. I'll talk to her. But I'm not going to promise anything."

Preeti's face broke open in a victorious big-sister grin. Peter tried not to let it irritate him.

"Wonderful! I know you will do your best." She closed the portfolio album and indicated it with a lifting motion. "Is it okay if I hang on to this for now?"

He gave a resigned sigh. "Sure. Knock yourself out."

She stood, and he did the same. Apparently, the interview was over. He swung his leather bomber-style jacket around him and slung his worn leather messenger bag over his shoulder. He headed for the glass doors of her office.

"Let me know by Friday," Preeti called after him.

"Not *promising* anything, Preeti," he tossed over his shoulder just before the door closed.

In spite of himself, he grinned.

He'd just been given another reason to talk to Melinda. This day just got better.

Preeti waited until the office door had closed behind her brother before she smiled. Templing her fingers, she examined the photo in front of her and thanked God for the stroke of fortune that had just landed in her lap. The girl who stared back at her from the page looked vulnerable and wise at the same time, like someone with secrets she kept close to her heart but yearned to share.

"Yes, you're perfect." Preeti picked up the album, meeting the girl's gaze.

One way or another, this girl would be in her magazine. She just didn't know it yet.

Chapter 9

MELINDA SAT AT HER kitchen table with her sewing machine pushed toward the wall and flipped through the album of eight-by-tens before her in amazement.

Peter sat on the apartment's only other chair across from her, directly below the studio shot of a smiling couple. He kept fidgeting with his clasped fingers as she examined his work, displaying an unusual amount of nerves. Melinda might have shown more empathy if her own anxiety level wasn't through the roof. She always felt that way when she knew she had to do something unpleasant.

And telling Peter she couldn't see him anymore was about the most unpleasant thing she could think of at the moment.

"These are amazing, Peter. Preeti's right—you are a very talented photographer."

Her memory of the photo shoot was a montage of hauling dresses and photographic lights around to various unlikely locations. She'd changed her clothes and hairstyle more times than she could count and contorted into what felt like the most unnatural poses—but they all looked completely natural and flattering in the photos before her. She could hardly believe the relaxed, happy, beautiful girl in the album was her. That day spent with Peter had been one of the most enjoyable she had had since . . . since Robert—

"So, I got the job," Peter said.

Melinda nodded. "I'm not surprised." She flipped pages slowly, mesmerized.

Why did these have to be so perfect?

Why did he?

MELINDA looked troubled. Peter couldn't figure out why. Did she not like the photos? She'd said she did, so it must be something else—that other thing that always lurked unsaid at the edges of every conversation. Maybe even the reason she didn't want to claim ownership of her own work.

This might not be the best time to dig deeper into Melinda's secrets, but he had given Preeti his word . . . and there may not ever be a *best time* for something like that, anyway. He leaned forward and rested his elbows on his knees, hands clasped in front of him.

"Melly, tell me the truth. Did you make those dresses?"

Melinda drew in a sharp breath and avoided his gaze for a few moments. Finally she sighed and straightened, meeting his eye.

"Yes," she said, resignation in her voice.

"Did you design them, too?"

"Yes," came the answer again.

"Well, that's great! They are beautiful—you obviously do a great job. And that's just coming from an uneducated dummy like me. Why didn't you say so before?"

A dark thought occurred to him.

"Robert doesn't . . . hurt you, does he?"

Melinda's gaze snapped to his. "What? No!"

Peter breathed a sigh of relief, the shook his head in confusion. "Then why?"

Melinda got up and started fiddling with the pins of the emerald-green and lemon-yellow frock printed with whimsical songbirds on the dress form.

Green? Birds? The alarms in her head screamed. *Why did that not clue me in?*

But she knew why she had taken such a dramatic departure from her typical fare. That week, she'd floated around the fabric store engulfed in a twitterpated euphoria, telling herself she was simply in the mood for something different. It was definitely time to cut ties while she still could . . . for Peter's sake.

"I didn't tell you before because of what you are doing now. I hate it when people make a big deal about me. I'm not a big deal. And I hate being in a spotlight. I just sew because . . . well, because it's what I do. It keeps me sane, and gives me something to do while Robert is away."

"I know you don't think so, but you actually are kind of a big deal," Peter said, half-smiling, but with a very intense look in his eyes. "Did you see those photos? I didn't have to use a lot of photographic skill to make the girl in them look fabulous. You are a natural model. I'm not the only one who believes so, either. Preeti loves those photos so much, she wants to hire you."

Melinda gaped at Peter in shock. "Me? What for?"

"Well, to model. But specifically, to model your own designs. She wants you to be the featured designer in their next issue."

Melinda felt like her brain had just experienced whiplash. She sank into the thrift-store vinyl chair, her thoughts spinning. *Preeti wants to hire me? But I'm not that good. Am I?* She twisted her ring.

"This could be a fantastic opportunity for you." His earnest black eyes pressed against her resolve. "You wouldn't have to work at the diner anymore. Preeti has a ton of connections in the fashion industry, and she could help you get set up doing this for a living. Wouldn't you like that?"

"Um, yes. I mean no." She shook her head. She had no credentials, no training. She was just a self-taught home sewer who liked to fiddle with pins and fabric in her spare time.

"Peter, I'm not a designer. And I'm not a model! Is this some kind of a joke?" She twisted her hands into her skirt and glared at him. Peter had taken his mischief too far this time. "I didn't think you would be so cruel."

"This is no joke, Melinda." He frowned. "Listen, you are a very beautiful woman, and it's time you know that Robert isn't the only man—uh, person—who thinks so. And look around! How many dresses do you have in that room? Fifty? A hundred?"

"One hundred forty-eight," she said mechanically, trying to process what was happening. If what he was saying were true, this could be her chance to start over, leave the past behind. She could—

"What? You see? You *are* a designer. And you create exactly the look *Fresh* wants. Preeti wanted to talk to you herself, but I thought you might take it better from me."

She blinked at him, the impact of his words hitting her with complete clarity. He *was* serious. She knew him well enough to decipher that much. But that was all the more reason to stick to her original plan. Working with *Fresh* would mean working with

Peter, and that absolutely must not be allowed to happen. Meeting his eyes, she wanted desperately to tell him she would do it, to not see disappointment etched on his beautiful face, but instead—

"I . . . I can't," she whispered.

"You can't what? Model? Be in the magazine?"

"None of it!" she said, surprising herself with her vehemence. "I can't be in the magazine, or be a designer, or see you anymore!"

Her volume had risen with each phrase, and she could feel her dam threatening to break open. Furiously, she knuckled the tears away and slammed the sluice gates shut on her emotions. Her will power nearly crumbled when she saw the stunned look on Peter's face.

"Melinda, you don't have to be in the magazine. No one is going to make you do anything you don't want to do. But—you don't want to be friends with me anymore? What did I do?"

Melinda looked away again, miserable. On the table, the open photograph showed her garbed in a retro skulls-and-roses print dress and surrounded by an opulent display of actual roses in a stunning array of colours. Her own smile mocked her.

"I just can't, Peter," she said in a low voice. "Thank you for the photos. Please leave."

She looked down at her hands, ignoring him ferociously, until he got up and grabbed his leather jacket from the back of the chair. Then he squatted directly in front of her so she had to work really hard not to meet his bottomless black eyes.

"Hurting you was the last thing I ever wanted to do, Melinda. Whatever I did, I'm sorry. I wish—" he broke off, then started again. His hand hovered inches from her face, but he slowly lowered it. "I'll go for now, but I'm not abandoning you. I'm your friend, and you won't get rid of me that easily."

When she didn't respond, he sighed, got up, and headed toward the door.

It was long after the apartment door clicked shut and the sound of his shoes descending the stairs had faded that she finally moved, pacing back and forth in the small space allowed by her tiny kitchen floor.

It was for Peter's own protection. She knew that. But that didn't make it hurt any less.

"Peter, I'm sorry," she murmured. "You'll never understand, I know that. It's just . . . everyone who gets close to me ends up dead."

Knowing she couldn't do any more sewing that evening, she crawled under the covers of her bed. The dam she'd built around her emotions burst wide open with a violence that shook the mattress on its frame.

Much later, when shuddering sighs were all that remained, she stumbled to the kitchen for a drink of water.

Staring up at her from the open book, the girl in

the photograph never even blinked. She was too engrossed with gazing at the person behind the camera with a wide, unguarded smile.

"HELLO, TransCan Airlines. How may I direct your call?" came the friendly female voice on the other end of the line.

"Uh, hi. My name is Peter Surati, and I am trying to get in contact with a pilot named Robert Clarkson. Would you be able to leave him a message for me?" asked Peter.

"One moment please."

Peter waited patiently, listening to keys clicking on the other end of the line.

"I'm sorry, sir, but there is no one by that name in our employee database. Are you certain that he works for our airline?"

"Well," Peter said, then hesitated. Suddenly he was not so certain. From the photo he had seen of Robert in a captain's uniform at Melinda's place, he knew he certainly had worked for that airline at one point. "He may have moved to a different airline, I suppose. Could you do an historical records check for me? It is extremely important that I get in contact with him."

"I'm sorry, sir, I don't have access to those files. I will put you through to the Human Resources department."

"Thank you."

After listening to a jazz rendition of a Broadway classic for about thirty seconds, a polite male voice came on the line.

"TransCan airlines, Andrew speaking. How may I help you?"

Peter explained his reason for calling again.

"I'm sorry, sir, those records are confidential."

Peter knew that laying on the charm would not work quite so well with a man as it would have with a woman. He tried a different approach.

"Mr. Clarkson has defaulted on a debt, and I represent Avery Collection Services. We are simply trying to track Mr. Clarkson down for our client."

The line was silent for a moment. "I can't give you any personal information about our employees. I am sorry I cannot be of more help."

Peter took a breath to keep from raising his voice in frustration. "Can you at least do a search to tell me how long ago he left your company? That might assist me in finding where he went next."

A pause on the line. "Let me check with my supervisor," Andrew said.

Before Peter could reply he was listening to an alto saxophone wail out an old Michael Bolton ballad. Blissfully, it was only a few seconds before the polite Andrew was back on the line.

"Mr. Surati?"

"Any luck?" Peter asked, trying to stop his brain from continuing where the song had been cut off. *Sometimes when we touch* . . .

Too late. He hated when songs got stuck in his head like that—especially the cheesy ones.

"That shouldn't violate any policy. One moment, please."

Keys clicked, then went silent.

I wanna hold you 'til I die . . .

Peter started singing one of his favourite Bollywood songs in Hindi in his head to obliterate the rest of the lyrics. Michael Bolton didn't stand a chance.

Andrew mumbled as he scanned the file, and Peter thought he caught the word *deceased*.

"Uh, Mr. Robert Clarkson has not worked for us for nearly three years. I can't tell you any more."

"Wait, did I hear you say he is deceased?" asked Peter. There was silence on the other end of the phone. "Andrew?"

"Yes, sir," came the reluctant reply.

"You're certain?" Peter asked, stunned, although knowing even as he said it that it was a foolish thing to say. That wasn't the sort of thing one joked about.

Andrew sighed. "Yes, sir. He died on December fourteen, three years ago. Is there anything else I can help you with, sir?"

"Uh, no. No, thank you. Have a good evening."

"Good evening, sir." The line went dead.

Peter put the phone down and rubbed his chin. What to do now? Was Robert really dead? It made sense in a way, since he never seemed to be around. And what about that wedding invitation? And if he were dead, why had she been pretending he wasn't? Some extreme form of denial?

He stood and started pacing.

Maybe it was the wrong Robert Clarkson. If only Melinda would talk to him, he wouldn't have to try to go through the back door to know for sure.

After leaving her so upset, he had told himself it was foolish to worry, that she had Robert to look after her, but still thought it would be best if he could touch base with the man. But now . . . what if she *didn't* have Robert? And if worries about a jealous fiancé weren't the reason she had broke off contact with him, then why did she?

He frowned. The obvious answer was that she simply didn't want him around anymore. Maybe he should respect that and walk away. She didn't owe him anything, after all.

He closed his eyes and rubbed his face. Unbidden, Kanti's face filled his vision. *Do you think I'm pretty, Peter?*

He drew in a breath. People didn't always know how to say what they meant. Especially people who were hurting. Maybe Melinda had been lying to him, or maybe she hadn't. And if she had, maybe she was simply trying not to be hurt again. Or maybe she'd decided she was better off alone.

But he didn't want her to be alone—not someone as special as she was. If Robert were truly dead, she'd remained faithful to him for three years since he'd passed. And a girl like that definitely deserved to know that there were those among the living who cared for her.

Without much hope, he punched in Melinda's phone number again.

She probably still wouldn't pick up. But he didn't know what else to do.

Chapter 10

MELINDA AND ROBERT WAITED anxiously in the hospital corridor as the doctor slipped silently out of her father's room and closed the door. Sounds of nurses and orderlies going about their duties filled the sterile space with soft rustles and muted murmurs. In the cancer ward, there weren't many loud noises, unless they were groans of pain or suffering.

The doctor was an older gentleman with a reassuring, grandfatherly manner, but right now, his face was grim.

"I'm sorry I don't have better news," he said. "The cancer has progressed more quickly than we expected. Your father is fighting hard, but he doesn't have much left to fight with. I'm afraid you need to expect the worst."

Melinda's hand covered her mouth, and her eyes were wide and moist.

Robert put his arm around her shoulders to steady her. "How long, Dr. Bezz?" he asked.

"It's possible that he has several more days. However, he most likely will not last the night. All we can really do now is to try and keep him comfortable."

After a history of robust health, Herman Myers had been diagnosed with liver cancer only three weeks before. He had gone into the emergency room with flu symptoms that seemed especially severe. By morning, they'd been told he had advanced liver cancer, and there was very little that could be done.

The weeks since the diagnosis had been a blur. The wedding which Melinda and Robert had been in the final stages of planning was put aside as she spent most of her days—and many of her nights—at the hospital. Others had come and gone with well-wishes for Herman's recovery, but only Robert's family, and Pastor Ralph McKay and his wife Edith really understood just how dire the situation was. Robert's sister Nadia had been by to sit with Melinda every few days, and Pastor Ralph had come to see his friend nearly as often, although Herman was seldom lucid enough for a visit. Sometimes Edith would come, too, just to make sure that Melinda was remembering to eat and give her a grandmotherly shoulder to cry on.

Robert had taken the last week off of work to spend time with her and relieve her from her bedside vigil so she could get some rest. But although she had barely slept and had lost considerable weight over the last month, her altered looks were nothing compared to the transformation she had watched her father go through. She would never have believed that three weeks could change someone's appearance so much, but as they entered the hospital room, the frail man on the bed seemed a cruel and ghostly caricature of the man who had been her pillar for the last sixteen years . . . since they had both lost the woman they loved most.

She sat down by his bed and touched his hand. The skin was yellowed and paper thin, crumpled like a glove that was too big for the hand it covered.

Herman's eyelids didn't even flicker.

"Hey, Dad," she said.

There was no response. Robert squeezed her shoulder and pulled over another uncomfortable, molded plastic chair to sit in. It made a horrible scraping noise on the tile floor that grated at her already-raw nerves.

The morphine they were administering to keep Herman comfortable made him sleep most of the time, but she and Robert still kept their voices low as they talked. They didn't say much, and when they did, it was always of the lightest topics possible— things far removed from the one thing their thoughts were centred on. Robert left and returned with a tea from the hospital cafeteria for her and a coffee for himself. Neither one of them would go home to sleep tonight.

After a nurse came in to check Herman's vitals, he stirred. His eyes opened and turned, unfocused, on his daughter, who grasped his hand in both of hers.

"Dad, can you hear me? I'm here. Robert is with me."

"Mindy? I'm . . . cold."

Melinda glanced at Robert, and he immediately went to get another warm blanket from the nurse's station. She turned back to her father, grieving at how his once-commanding face now sagged slack and uncertain. Suddenly, his features firmed and his steel-grey eyes looked right into Melinda's face.

"I'm sorry I'm going to miss your wedding, honey. I really wanted to give you away."

Tears slid down Melinda's face, but she ignored them. "It's okay, Dad. At least you'll get to sit with Mom for the ceremony."

She forced a smile, and saltwater brined her tongue. He weakly gripped her hand back.

"Robert is a good man. At least I can go, knowing that you will be looked after."

"Daddy?" she whimpered, though she hadn't called him that for years. "I don't want you to go."

Her body shook with sobs and her head dropped to her chest. He placed his other hand on hers, the one with the IV tube taped to the back. The palm was warm and reassuring against her skin.

"You'll be all right," he said, patting her hand.

Robert returned with a nurse, who began arranging a warmed flannel sheet over the several other blankets already covering her father.

Herman's gaze flicked around and encompassed Robert. "You'll be all right," he repeated. "Always remember I love you."

With that, his eyes closed and he slipped into unconsciousness. By morning, his body had been moved to the hospital morgue.

She went through most of the next week in a trance, completely numb. After the buckets of tears she had shed while her father went through his ordeal, she thought she had cried every last tear she could muster.

Robert was there through all the funeral preparations and paperwork that ensued. He just held and comforted her, not making her talk or offering platitudes like so many of the well-wishers who came to the funeral or sent flowers or cards. But when the funeral was over and the people stopped coming, Robert finally had to go back to work. She didn't want to be left alone, but she knew it was necessary.

Two weeks later, Melinda prepared to greet Robert after five days away. Her hair and makeup were partly done, and she was already dressed in her surprise for him—the first sewing project she had made since the skirt with her mother, a dress finished only that afternoon. Opening her favourite lipstick, she was startled by the jangle of the telephone. Glancing at the clock, she thought it must be Robert——maybe his flight had come in early and he was calling to let her know.

If only.

"It's Nadia," came the urgent voice on the other end of the line. "Turn on the news."

Confused, she turned on the TV, the phone still at her ear. A newscaster was outlining what was known about a commercial plane that had gone down over the mountains only an hour before. She sank onto the couch, the phone falling from her hand.

As the flight number was announced, she uttered a soundless, "Oh, no."

She was still sitting on the couch two hours later, eyes riveted to the news broadcast in desperate shock, when Robert's mother Valerie called her with the news—forced out with a shaking voice—that Robert had not been among the survivors.

MELINDA was jolted back to the present by the shrill ring of the telephone. She didn't stir from her chair as the answering machine kicked on and Nadia's voice came on the line.

"Hi, Mel. Thinking of you today. I want you to

know I'm still here if you ever want to talk. Oh, uh, Jason and I will be in the city on the weekend, and we hoped you would join us for dinner." Pause. "I miss you, girl, and I love you. Please call me back."

The machine clicked off. Immediately, the phone started ringing again. It wasn't like Nadia to be this persistent. Tightening her jaw, Melinda went into the bathroom to brush her teeth, but opened it a crack when she heard Peter's voice come on the line.

"Hi, Melinda, it's Peter. Please pick up. I know you're there. I stopped by the diner earlier, and Sandra told me you were home sick."

That was true—she had taken the day off, as she did every anniversary of her father's passing.

There was a pause for a few seconds.

"Melly, I really want to talk to you. I'm . . . well, I'm worried about you. Whatever you're going through right now, you don't have to do it alone. You know that, right?" He sighed into the phone. "Call me back when you get this. Please."

Pause. Click.

Melinda dropped the toothbrush into the holder and crawled under the covers. This was the second Friday in a row that the emerald-and-lemon bird dress had hung in a half-finished pinned state on the dress form. She hadn't touched it since the night she'd sent Peter packing.

In fact, she didn't know if she would ever sew

again.

Chapter 11

Peter turned the key in his mailbox to lock it closed, then started rifling through the handful of envelopes, bills, and flyers. The latest issue of his photography magazine had come. He headed toward the apartment stairs, relishing the thought of perusing it over a cup of coffee.

On the third step, he paused—there was an envelope with his name and address written in Preeti's hand, but with Fresh printed in the return address. Using his pinky finger as a letter opener, he jaggedly ripped open the envelope and pulled out a cheque. A handwritten note from his sister said simply, "For photography services rendered." She hadn't even signed it.

Confused, he looked in the envelope for a letter or some other explanation, but it was empty. He had already received payment for the relaunch gig, and had not yet done any other work for the magazine, so he had no idea what this cheque could be for. Some kind of advance, maybe?

Peter speed-dialled Preeti's cell number and held his phone to his ear with his shoulder as he unlocked the apartment door and entered, tossing his keys and the other mail on a side table by the door as he came in. When he heard the line click open, he started in right away.

"Hey, Preeti, do you know—?"

A polite message in his sister's contralto voice cut him off.

"You have reached Preeti Anderson's cell phone. Leave a message, and I'll call you back as soon as I can." *Beep*.

"Hey, Preeti, just got this cheque from *Fresh*, but I'm not quite sure what it is for. Give me a call when you can, okay?"

Peter clicked his phone closed and tossed the cheque on top of the pile of mail, then went rummaging through the refrigerator for leftover takeout. Digging out some cold Kung Pao chicken, he ate it straight from the carton and went to stand in front of his computer monitor to contemplate what he'd unearthed.

On the screen was an article he'd found last night about Robert Clarkson, a pilot who had died in a plane crash almost three years ago. The man's photo was inset into the text.

It was definitely the same Robert.

THE next morning was Monday. December second.

In India, December had been a welcome reprieve from the heat of summer and the wetness of monsoon. However, since moving to Calgary, Peter disliked December. Not only was the weather becoming intolerably cold—which seemed to penetrate even the warmest of winter gear to chill his Mumbai-grown bones—but the Alberta air was always dry, and became even more so when the little remaining humidity crystallized into solid form on the ground. As he made his deliveries, the constant in-and-out of the warmed truck made his nose run and his throat crack.

He dropped the box from *Fresh* on the receiving desk of Chapters bookstore and handed his digital pen and signature pad to the receiving clerk. While he waited for her to sign off, he stamped his feet to warm up.

"Cold enough for ya?" She chuckled.

It was a question he heard often on his rounds when the weather was like this, and he had come to learn it was the polite way that Canadians had of commiserating about the weather without appearing to complain about it. He wasn't sure if he had hit on the appropriate response, yet, but he thought as long as it was humorous, what he actually said probably didn't matter much.

"If I never saw freezing again, let alone twenty below, it would be too soon," Peter replied good-naturedly.

Laughing, the curly-haired woman handed back his pad and pen. As he turned to leave, she grabbed a utility knife to split the plastic binding on the box.

"Stay warm!" she called after him.

He waved in response to this other oft-heard greeting and stepped through the heavy metal door into the unforgiving winter air.

He swung into his truck and checked his next stop. He was making good time. Maybe he'd stop at Fred's Diner for lunch today. Melinda would have a hard time avoiding him there.

She doesn't owe you anything.

Except an explanation, maybe.

His phone rang, and his sister's number showed on the call display. He punched the Answer button.

Maybe he'd get more than one explanation today.

"Awesome," said the curly-haired woman to no one in particular as she opened the box to the latest edition of *Fresh*. "I've been waiting for these."

She grabbed a stack of magazines to take out and inspect. She'd barely glanced at the tantalizing cover image when her supervisor called her over with a question.

"Coming, Bob!" she yelled back, placing the bundle of glossy magazines down on the desk.

When the clerk came back to her station and slit the plastic straps that bound the bundle together, the cover caught her eye. She peered at the pensive woman with her dark hair piled high on her head in a retro style that emphasized her aquiline neck. She wore a fabulously chic charcoal-grey sheath dress. Set in eye-grabbing fonts, the headline read, "The Surprising Melinda Myers: From Fashion Oblivion to Centre Stage".

The clerk flipped to the title story and to ogle over the dresses that were the brainchild of the up-and-coming local designer. Idly, she wondered what the chances were of ever meeting Ms. Myers, and where she could find a dress like that one with the red embroidered rose-and-thorn pattern for the staff Christmas party.

At another shout from her boss, she jumped to her feet, grabbed the box of magazines and started for the front end to stock shelves.

It was a particularly snowy winter already. More than once, bus routes had been delayed because of poor road conditions, and even though Melinda walked part of the way to work for exercise, she didn't always allow enough extra time for the amount of effort it took to slog through drifts up to her knees that had not yet been cleared. This Tuesday was one of those days, and when she finally stamped the snow off of her boots on the black rubber doormat of Fred's Diner and changed into her work shoes, she knew without looking at the retro chrome-accented clock above the counter that she was late.

Sandra was huddled over a magazine laid out on the counter, wet rag forgotten in her hand as she whispered excitedly with Margot, one of the morning line cooks. Fred's wasn't due to open for another twenty minutes, but that still didn't usually leave much time for the opening staff to dally with small talk. When Melinda opened the inner set of doors and the chimes jingled, the two women stopped chattering and looked up at her in a most peculiar way. Sandra was wearing a smile that she usually only reserved for her big tippers.

"Morning, Melinda. Did you have a good weekend?"

"Same as always," she replied, her face stony as she swept by toward the door to the back of the restaurant. Out of politeness, she forced herself to enquire, "You?"

"Oh, you know. It's always a little crazy running the kids here, there, and everywhere, 'specially in this weather. I survived, though. 'Course, I don't think any news I have could really compare to yours, no matter what you pretend, Miss 'Ain't-Nothing-Happening-Here'."

Melinda stopped in her tracks, confused. "What do you mean?"

"Why, *this*, sweet pea, and don't act like you're not excited about it. I swear, sometimes you wouldn't take a compliment if the good Lord Above came and handed it to ya wrapped in a pretty red bow. This is amazing!"

Sandra shoved the open magazine into Melinda's face, and Melinda's mittens, purse, and boots all crashed to the floor with a loud thump.

There she was, in full glossy with tiny paragraphs and flowing subtitles on each page. She snatched the magazine from Sandra and quickly flipped through page after page of herself posing in her dresses, then looked at the front. *Fresh*. Of course.

"Myers, I need to talk to you," growled Fred through the pass-through window. "My office. Now."

Melinda handed the magazine back to Sandra in a stunned daze and shuffled back to Fred's tiny office as if in a trance. The desk, which was built into one short end of the small rectangular room, was neat and tidy, office supplies contained in utilitarian organizers, with a stack of file folders in one corner. Fred closed the door behind her and wiped his hands on the mostly white apron around his waist. At this time of day, there hadn't been much to smear it yet.

Fred ran a hand over his bald head, looking like he was trying to figure out how to phrase something unpleasant. "Myers, I've given you chance after chance. You were doing pretty good there for a while, you know? I thought this was going ta work out after all. But lately, you been moping 'round here like you're on a solid diet of lemons and Prairie Oysters. What's going on? You feeling okay?"

Melinda shook her head, barely seeing Fred. How could Peter have sold his photos of her when she had expressly told him they were only for his portfolio?

"No, I'm not. In fact, I feel quite ill. I think I better go home."

She wasn't exaggerating—her head was spinning so fast, she sank into the rolling office chair in a daze. The scowl on Fred's round, clean-shaven face slid into a furrowed brow full of concern. He whipped off his apron and hung it on a peg on the back of the office door, then grabbed his coat and keys.

"I'll take ya home, then. You do look pretty awful. Caught that flu that was going 'round, didja? Why'd ya even come inta work today?"

He opened the office door and hollered toward the kitchen. "Wong!"

Margot's head popped around the corner.

"Finish setting up for me," Fred barked. "I'm taking Melinda home. Be back in half an hour."

Margot gave an efficient nod and disappeared into

the bowels of the kitchen again.

Melinda protested that she could get herself home, but Fred insisted, and she didn't fight very hard. She really did feel physically ill at the moment, and the thought of fighting her way home through all those drifts—against the wind, this time—followed by the morning crush in transit persuaded her . . . despite the fact that it meant spending fifteen minutes in a vehicle with her gruff-natured employer. She stumbled out of the office after him.

"Hey, Melinda, where can I get a dress like this one?" Sandra asked as Melinda passed the counter on the way to the front door, pointing at a photo in the magazine with a red-lacquered fingernail. "My daughter is graduating this year, and she would look fabulous in it."

"Back to work, White!" Fred shouted as he marched briskly toward the front doors. He punched the Command Start button on his key fob, and a car engine outside revved to life. "And call Lacey to cover!"

"I—I don't know," Melinda said, practically fleeing through the door behind Fred.

The cheerful clang of the bell chased her out with its mocking laughter.

"Preeti! What were you thinking?" exclaimed Peter, shaking the magazine in his sister's face.

They were once again in the uncomfortable white office, and Peter was leaning on the disconcerting glass desk as his sister sat—unperturbed, hands folded, smiling up at him infuriatingly—on the other side.

"Melinda didn't agree to this. *I* didn't agree to this. This isn't even legal!"

"You had her sign the standard modelling release form, did you not?"

"Yes, but—"

"Then she didn't have to agree to it. The article may have been more interesting had she allowed herself to be interviewed, mind you, but her photos can be used in any way you want."

"But I didn't agree to this! Those are *my* photos, Preeti. And I would never have let you use them without Melinda's consent."

"You're an employee of *Fresh* now, aren't you? Okay, subcontractor, not employee. Any photos you submit to us are free to be used in our magazine."

"I didn't submit those. They were in my portfolio. Preeti, you have really gone too far this time."

With a grunt of frustration, he threw the magazine on her desk and started pacing the office, trying hard not to punch the wall. They were mostly glass, so that would not have ended well.

"While technically, you didn't submit those for our use, they *are* here." Her calm tone only goaded him further. "I was actually doing both you and Melinda a favour, you know. I'm surprised you don't see it. And you were paid, as she will be for modelling when you give her this."

Preeti reached into her desk drawer and pulled out a white envelope. It had the *Fresh* logo and return address printed on the top left corner, but only *Melinda Myers* and no forwarding address written on it in Preeti's hand. She smiled and held out the envelope.

"Are you going to sue me, Peter?"

Glaring, he snatched it from her, then yanked a pen from the organizer on her desk. On the back of the envelope, he scrawled Melinda's address.

"Give it to her yourself, and explain what you did—that I had nothing to do with it. She already doesn't want to talk to me. And here. You can have this back."

He reached into his shirt pocket and pulled out the folded cheque from *Fresh*, ripped it in half and let the pieces fall in front of her. Snatching up his portfolio from where it sat on the edge of her desk, he said, "I quit." And left.

Preeti sighed. She tossed the discarded pieces of torn paper in the garbage bin and picked up the envelope, regarding it thoughtfully. After a moment, she pulled out a fresh one and began to write the address information in its proper location on the blank face so it could be mailed. Then she stopped and pursed her lips, tapping the pen against them.

She had never seen Peter that upset with her in her life. Not even when they were teenagers and she had told Chanda Ravuraj that Peter had a huge crush on her and was going to ask her out—which might have been true, who knows?

The crush part was not exaggerated, at any rate. Word had gotten back to Chanda's father, who was outraged by "that forward Surati boy," as was their own father when Mr. Ravuraj came to discuss the matter with him. It had taken days to sort it all out, but after the dust settled, Peter cooled off and they were fine again. That was how their disputes usually went, but something told Preeti that this time, things were different.

With a rare twinge of guilt, she tucked the un-opened envelope with Melinda's address on the back into her purse. She would stop by the girl's apartment right after work and get this whole mess sorted out.

Then, without another thought, Preeti turned back to reviewing story ideas for next issue's fashion pages.

Chapter 12

MELINDA SAT IN THE middle of her living room floor—something she hadn't seen in over a year—with a pile of flattened dress boxes on one side and scores of dresses laid in several piles on the couch on the other. She had been tempted to leave the couch bare, since it was such a novelty to be able to sit on it again, but she reminded herself that it would be available full-time once her task was complete. She stood up to survey her progress.

Some of the dresses she had unboxed—the ones she loved the most and was the most proud of—were now hanging in her no-longer-barren closet. It felt strange to take ownership of the fact, but she was proud of her work. Each dress was a milestone passed, a design lesson learned, a vision transformed into reality. At the time she had made these gowns, she had simply been driven by the need to create, to keep busy . . . to forget. The end result had been of little consequence, and had received equally little thought after its single use on her "date night" with Robert. Until now.

After a quick jaunt to the kitchen to stretch her legs and grab a drink of water, she settled back down on the living room floor to finish sorting the last pile of boxes. The dresses that emerged from their cardboard hideaways were sorted into Sell, Keep, or Give Away piles, and the accompanying patterns were filed into a box for posterity.

Going through the boxes had been like peeling up layers on an archaeological dig. As she had figuratively moved backward through time in her fashion journey, the dresses had shifted from mostly going into the closet or the Sell pile to being almost exclusively put into the Give Away pile. She was glad for the lessons learned from those early dresses, but they paled in comparison to her more recent work.

Finally, Melinda reached the last box. She opened it and hesitated, then slowly pulled out the first dress she had ever made—the one she had meant to surprise Robert with on the fourteenth of December three years ago. It was a simple polyester crepe sheath dress in blush pink. She cringed a little as she examined the sloppy, uneven darts and the mismatched zipper. She had machine-stitched the hem, not wanting to take the time required for an invisible hand-done job, and the hem stitch wasn't even straight. Still . . . it was the only dress she had ever truly intended to wear on a date with Robert.

On the day he died.

She clambered to her feet, intending to hang the First Dress in her closet.

The intercom buzzed.

"Melinda? Let me in. Please?"

Melinda hesitated in front of the speaker, intense anger at the man with the clipped Indian accent warring with other emotions. Her hand came halfway up to press the admittance button, then froze in midair.

She didn't want to see Peter. No, definitely not. She had firmly decided this was for the best, and she needed to stay the course.

She let her hand drop.

PETER was about to buzz Melinda again when another resident of the apartment building came out of the locked door and politely held it open for him. Smiling his thanks, he dashed through and leapt up the stairs, two at a time, to her second-floor apartment.

MELINDA had just turned away from the intercom to continue toward her bedroom when she heard a man's tread echoing on the stairs, then the stairwell door crashing open, and then—while she stood frozen, hoping for and against the inevitable—a knock on her door.

"Melinda? Are you in there? Melinda? Please let me in. I really need to talk to you."

Melinda stared at the door and didn't move.

"Fine, I just need you to listen, anyway. First of all, I am really sorry about what happened with *Fresh*. I never wanted to hurt you, and I hope you believe I had nothing to do with publishing those pictures."

Melinda's brow furrowed and her mouth twisted. He hadn't told them to publish the photos? Was he telling the truth? There was a rhythmic swooshing in her ears, but she still didn't move.

ONE of the other apartment tenants brushed past Peter on her way down the hallway. Peter leaned against Melinda's door and waited until the woman was out of earshot before he continued.

"I—I know you've been lying to me about Robert. I found his obituary and an article about the crash online. I just don't know why you didn't tell me. And I don't know what I did to offend you, either. Well, until this magazine thing came up, anyway. Arg!"

Peter ran a hand over his mouth in frustration. He was doing this all wrong, but he didn't know how to do it any better. He was pretty sure Melinda was listening to every word, since Sandra at the diner had told him how Fred had taken Melinda home first thing that morning. But still, maybe she wasn't.

He reached into his messenger bag and grabbed a pen and the article he had printed out about the crash that killed Robert. Quickly, he scribbled something across the blank reverse side of the page, then slid it under the door to the apartment. With a final look at the door, he sighed and turned back toward the stairs.

THE silence stretched. Melinda took a hushed step to peek through the peephole to see if Peter was still standing there. She couldn't see anything.

Printer pages were shoved under the door. She jumped, stifling a squeak of surprise with her hands. She held her breath. A few seconds later, Peter sighed in exasperation and left.

Cautiously, she bent to pick up the papers.

She remembered the article well. The exact same one was tucked into the side table in her room, snipped out of the newspaper when it had been printed. Still, she scanned the words quickly, surprised at how calmly she was able to read it now—she didn't even have to blink back tears.

Not until she turned the last page and deciphered what Peter had scribbled so hastily on the back in black ink.

Melly, I'm so sorry. Hurting you is the last thing I wanted to do. Please let me explain everything, and then you can hate me for the rest of your life if you want. Just let me try, because I really want you not to hate me. Peter.

Wiping her eyes, she was surprised to find the rose-coloured dress still draped over her arm. She laid the pages, reverse-side-up, on the counter on top of the dusty wedding invitation, and then returned to the living room. The pink sheath dress was the final article to land on the Give pile.

She gave it one last regretful look, but left it where it was and started packing the dresses into bags to take to their next destination.

"I'm sorry, Robert," she said to the smiling man in the engagement photo as she took the rustic wooden frame off the end of the upper cabinets. "I may not be quite ready to move on. But I know that I have to let you go. It's time for me to start living again."

As an afterthought, she also dug out the wedding invitation from where it hid under Peter's note.

She laid the photo in a shoebox with several others and slipped the invitation down beside it. The image of Robert's handsome face in the photograph smiled at her, as always, and seemed to nod his approval. She smiled back. Then she placed the thick envelope containing her engagement ring wrapped in tissue on top of the photo and slid the box under her bed.

Chapter 13

MELINDA RAPPED ON THE minister's open office door. "Pastor McKay?"

An elderly gentleman with a fringe of white hair looked up from his desk. His pale blue eyes widened.

"Melinda! Melinda Myers." A warm smile flooded his face as he stood up to greet her. He clasped her small hand in his wide one. "Come in, come in!"

He indicated the padded chair on the other side of his desk for her to sit in. She thanked him, settled herself in the chair and unbuttoned her coat, and slung her purse onto the carpeted floor by her feet.

Pastor McKay folded his hands on the desk in front of him. "To what do I owe the pleasure?"

Melinda stared at him, fighting a surge of emotion. She had sat under Pastor McKay's teaching most Sundays during her childhood and teenage years. He was the pastor who had buried her mother,

her father, and who was supposed to marry her and Robert. Pastor Ralph McKay and his late wife, Edith, had spent more than a few Sunday afternoons fellowshipping in the Myers' home. In fact, he was the closest thing she had to a grandfather that she could remember. However, after her father, and then Robert, had passed away, she had stopped attending church, managing to shut Pastor McKay and the rest of the church family of her youth out, just like everyone else she had ever cared about.

Seeing him now, she resisted the urge to hug him.

"It's really good to see you, Pastor McKay." She gave him a hesitant but genuine smile. "I know it's been a long time."

She twisted her fingers in a tight knot, then took a breath.

"I came here today because I have a question that I am hoping you can answer."

He nodded. "I will do what I can. What's troubling you, child?"

Another deep breath, and then she dove in. "Can someone be . . . cursed?" She searched his face to see his reaction.

Ralph McKay put his elbows on his desk, clasping his hands under his chin and regarding her thoughtfully. "What kind of a curse are you asking about?"

"Well, could someone be cursed, say, to not be allowed to be close to anyone? Or to have those close to them be in danger, possibly mortal danger?"

It sounded kind of silly when she said it out loud—even to her own ears—but she needed to know.

If it were possible, it would confirm her suspicions. Maybe she could become a hermit, move to the Northwest Territories and live off the land like the Inuit, so she wouldn't endanger anyone else ever again. But if it *weren't* . . . She barely dared to hope, or breathe, as she waited for a response from the man of the cloth for whom she had so much respect.

"I can think of several instances in the Old Testament where God cursed the families of someone who had rebelled against him, and they all died. In those cases, the family members themselves were also usually living in rebellion to God, so the punishment was just for all."

Melinda let out a breath she didn't realize she had been holding, her shoulders slumping. She nodded slowly in resignation.

"I thought so."

She lifted her purse and stood to go in one fluid motion.

"Wait, Melinda. Please." Pastor McKay held out his hand. "I'm not finished, child."

Melinda turned back toward him, but didn't sit down.

"Do you think you are under such a curse?" His kind eyes held hers with a steady and concerned gaze.

With tight lips, she nodded.

"I see," he said, leaning back in his chair. "And why would you think that?"

"Because," she mumbled, and her voice cracked.

"Pardon?" He leaned forward to hear her better. "These old ears aren't what they used to be."

She cleared her throat.

"Because I walked away from God," she said. "I was angry with him, and refused to serve him anymore."

"Hmm. And when did this most horrible act of rebellion against God occur?" he challenged her gently. "The one that condemned Robert, the god-fearing man you loved, to death? Or your father, who served as a deacon in this very church and set an example of humility and charity to all who knew him?"

Melinda's shoulders were still slumped, and she couldn't meet his gaze. Her carefully constructed dam was cracking. Emotions she'd held back for years rose in her like a watery tide. She balled her hands into fists, trying to maintain control.

"But you were only seven—or was it six?—years old when your mother died," Pastor McKay continued. "Was it still in the tender years of your childhood that you turned your back on your maker, thus bringing down his wrath on you and all of those dear to you?"

Melinda's barriers cracked. He was right. How

could she not have seen it? God hadn't abandoned her. She had abandoned him, too angry to seek his face any longer. With a heaving sob, she started weeping and fell back into the chair, covering her face with her hands.

Pastor McKay shuffled around the desk to sit in the chair next to her and placed a comforting hand on her shoulder.

"Child, I have known you from the moment your dear mother gave birth to you. I watched you grow up, and was with you through your darkest hours. I know that it was only *after* you lost those most precious to you that you became angry with God and turned away. It's okay—he is not upset by your anger. He loves you still, and is calling you back. You know that, don't you?"

Melinda did. Like someone had turned on the sun, she finally saw the gaping cavern of loneliness in her spirit for what it was—not an ache to be in Robert's arms, or even to see her father or mother. From beyond the bottomless black cavern she'd been living in, she could hear the Spirit's call—*Come back to the Father*, it said. *Come back to Me.*

But she was not quite ready.

Through her tears, she whimpered in agony, "Then why did they die?"

Pastor Ralph sighed and patted her shoulder soothingly as she wept. "I can't tell you that for certain. The only one who can answer that question is the Father himself. But I know it was not out of malicious intent toward you, child. He loves you more than life, which is why his own son, Jesus, died on that cross so long ago—to redeem you, so that you can go live with him eventually. Your mother believed that, as did your father and Robert . . ."

He sighed.

"Maybe God took them simply because it was time for them to come home."

Melinda's tears were quieter now, but she still sat with her face covered, sniffling. Pastor McKay handed her a box of tissue, which she took gratefully.

"Why don't you take some quiet time in the sanctuary and talk to your heavenly Father about this?" he invited. "No one will bother you there. I will be right here if you need anything."

Melinda nodded and then stood, taking her purse and the tissue with her.

Before she stepped out of the office, she paused. "Thank you, Pastor McKay."

He smiled gently. "Welcome home, Melinda."

Over a week later, Melinda crunched across the snow to her apartment building, head still reeling from the events of the afternoon as she fumbled in her purse for her keys.

She had taken a cab to the upscale commission

clothing store downtown where she had dropped off about two dozen of the dresses from the Sell stash she'd accumulated the previous Tuesday. When she called the store that morning to see if any of the dresses had moved and ask if they were ready for more, the lady on the other end of the phone laughed at her incredulously.

"Moved!" she barked in a tone that seemed at odds with her proper British accent. "Why didn't you tell me you were the Melinda Myers who's on the cover of that hoity-toity ladies' magazine? After the first couple disappeared before I could say 'Sally's your aunt,' with both buyers commenting on the bargain prices for 'a Melinda Myers original', we put up the price for the rest of them. You better get on down here, dearie, and bring the whole kit and caboodle, whatever you've got left."

When Melinda got to the store, there was a giant-sized enlargement of the current cover of *Fresh* in the window, and a hand-written sign in block letters made with Magic Marker that read *Now carrying Melinda Myers!*

Her disbelief only increased when she got inside and the stately shopkeeper informed her that only one of the previous dresses remained. The stylish, matronly woman eagerly took the dresses Melinda had brought with her, expressing genuine admiration as she hung them on a clothes rack one by one to be steamed and displayed later.

"Ladies have been asking if we can get these in other sizes. Is that possible?"

Melinda shook her head in astonishment. "I, um, I don't know. Let me think about it."

After all the dresses had been hung, the stout woman reached behind the counter and pulled out an envelope with Melinda's name on the front.

"Here are your earnings, dearie."

Melinda opened the flap, which wasn't sealed, and glanced at the figure on the cheque. She gaped.

"How is this possible?"

Surely all of the dresses together could not have sold for so much, let alone her commissions on the first dozen. It was more than she made waitressing in almost two months!

"We ended up selling most of those dresses for over four hundred dollars each." The shopkeeper placed her hands on the counter and her voice took on a mothering tone. "Dearie, I'm glad you brought these to my store, but you really ought to consider going into business for yourself. You are a very talented designer."

Melinda was still mulling those words over as she reached for the handle on the front door of her building.

"Melinda! Ms. Myers!" a woman's voice called from behind her, and she paused.

Looking around, she saw Preeti jogging awkwardly toward her in high-heeled leather boots from the curb where a cab sat waiting. Melinda held the door open and let the fashionably but impractically dressed woman enter the lobby ahead of her.

"Thanks for waiting," Preeti said brightly.

"I have nothing to say to you."

Melinda crossed her arms over her chest and stared down at the other woman, whose smile faded. Even in heels and with Melinda in her flat, warm snow boots, Preeti was a very short woman.

"I . . . guess I deserve that. Look, I just came to give you this. Sorry it took so long."

She handed Melinda an envelope with her own name on the front in a neat woman's script, and her address on the back in the same hurried hand Peter had used for the note sitting on her kitchen counter.

"It's a cheque. And . . . I also want to say I'm sorry. I did not mean to cause problems for you. Believe it or not, it was because I believed in your talent—and Peter's—that I printed that article. I truly wanted to help you both. And you wouldn't believe the positive feedback we've been getting. People really love your work, Ms. Myers."

Melinda's arms remained crossed for a moment, and then she begrudgingly took the envelope. "*You* did it? Peter didn't tell you to print those photos?"

"No." She gave a snorting laugh. "In fact, he was

quite perturbed about the whole thing, threatened never to speak to me again, et cetera. You know, typical baby brother tantrum."

Peter had been telling the truth! Warmth flooded her. But that didn't mean she forgave his sister.

Melinda eyed the other woman coldly. "No, I don't, actually."

Preeti hesitated. "Of course not. Sorry. Well, I guess it's actually good that it took me a week to get over here, because now I also have this to give you."

She handed over another envelope made from high-quality linen paper. Melinda's heart sped up when she saw the logo of a well-known Toronto-based design company on the return address.

"Madame Bouvier recommended you to them. From what she told me on the phone, they would like to discuss bringing you on as another design partner. You must have made quite the impression at the gala." Preeti arched a brow.

Melinda blinked. She took the envelope and nodded. "Anything else?"

"Yes, there is, actually." Preeti hesitated, then hurried on in a rush. "Peter hasn't dated many girls, but the few he has have usually broken his heart. Still, I've never seen him as torn up as he has been for the last couple of weeks. I'm pretty sure the reason is you. I know you most likely have your reasons, and I don't mean to pry, but please . . . would you call him?

Let him get some closure? I don't want to see him wrecked because of a girl he didn't even date. He is much too decent of a man for that."

Melinda's throat closed. She couldn't say anything, so she nodded.

"Don't wait too long. His phone number is only good until Sunday."

"Why?"

"He took a photography job in Vancouver. He's moving."

Melinda's heart felt like it had stopped. She stared at Preeti with her mouth hanging open, unable to speak. *That's only two days away!*

Preeti put her leather-gloved hands in her pockets and shifted her feet. "Okay. Well, I think I have taken up enough of your time. Goodbye, Ms. Myers."

She stepped out the door, taking careful steps on the icy sidewalk until she climbed back into the waiting cab.

While ascending the single flight of stairs to her apartment, Melinda's head reeled as though she had been struck. She left the envelopes, forgotten, on top of the counter and sank onto the couch, stunned.

Because she now knew two things for certain—Peter had loved her. And although she now knew it was safe to love him back, it might be too late.

Chapter 14

ON SATURDAY, DECEMBER FOURTEENTH, Melinda awoke early, her stomach already balled into knots. After she had calmed down the previous evening, she had made two phone calls and then gotten to work sewing. Even though she had been awake well into the wee hours of the morning, nerves and habit still woke her up at six o'clock. But she had no intention of going to work today.

Her original plan for the day was to stay home, stay in bed, and hide from the world. She had taken the day off weeks ago with that exact intention, knowing that trying to work on the anniversary of Robert's death would have been completely impossible for her. But yesterday, her plans had changed.

Quickly, she got dressed in the emerald-and-lemon bird-printed dress that had kept her up so late. It had been so long since she had worn anything but monochromatic tones, or the robin's-egg blue waitressing uniform, that she took a moment to admire the effect on her complexion. Her cheeks looked rosy, but she suspected that was also because of nerves.

An hour later, she was sipping tea at her kitchen table, ready to go. It was much too early to leave, and she tried to calm down by reading. When she realized that she had re-read the exact same page for the third time and still not comprehended a word, she gave up and closed the book.

She checked the clock again. Seven-thirty. *That's late enough.* She called a cab.

At precisely 7:59 a.m., she buzzed Peter's apartment from the foyer of his building.

"Melinda? You're very early for a Saturday," said a groggy-sounding Peter through the intercom. The door clicked and buzzed, and Melinda went in.

When Peter answered the door, he was dressed in jeans and a white T-shirt and breathing hard, as if he had been running. Melinda noted with amusement that his socks were mismatched and his hair a bit rumpled, but other than that, he gave no sign of how unprepared she knew he must have been for her early arrival. He had been expecting her—just maybe not before ten a.m.

"Tea?" he asked as she struggled out of her boots.

"Yes, thank you," she said, relieved that she would have a prop to help her through the upcoming conversation, something to focus on. Her stomach clenched, and she took a deep, steadying breath as she hung up her coat. The room smelled like leather and stale Indian food.

While Peter fiddled around in the kitchen, Melinda settled onto his couch and smoothed the skirt of her dress, looking around. The apartment was fairly tidy and tastefully decorated in muted, rich colours, accented with polished wood sculptures and art that bore the exotic flair of Peter's home country. Photography books decorated the heavy, glass-topped wooden coffee table in front of her, and on the far wall she spotted a dark wooden bookshelf next to the TV. She tilted her head and scanned the titles—John Grisham and Clive Cussler novels, books titled in a strange script that she thought must be Hindi, and a few engineering textbooks.

Peter set a heavy stoneware mug of Indian-style boiled chai tea in front of her on the elegantly-carved table, and then settled himself into an overstuffed leather chair on the other side.

"I didn't know you liked John Grisham." She picked up the steaming mug and blew across it—she didn't like tea to scald her tongue when she drank it.

He glanced at the bookshelf and shrugged.

"There are a lot of things you don't know about me," he said simply, but not accusingly. He drew in a deep breath. "Listen, Melly—uh, Melinda, about those photos. I—"

She held up her hand to shush him and shook her head. "Preeti explained everything," she said. "I know it's not your fault."

His features became unreadable. "Oh," was all he said, lapsing into a silence that soon began to stretch uncomfortably.

"Preeti also told me you are moving to Vancouver," Melinda said finally, forcing herself to meet his eyes as she spoke. She refused to hide from him any longer.

"Yep," Peter acknowledged with a shrug, nodding.

"I've been offered a position at a design house in Toronto," she said.

"Really? That's great. Really, really great."

When he didn't add anything, Melinda decided it was time to bite the bullet.

"I thought it was my fault. That Robert died, I mean."

Peter's eyes widened momentarily and he sat up at the sudden topic change. Then his brow furrowed in reaction to the statement she made.

"Why would you think it was your fault?" he asked.

"This might sound strange, but I need to tell you all of it, so can you bear with me?"

He nodded quietly, studying her.

She took another deep breath to slow her heart,

then began.

"When I found out Robert was going on that five-day run, I really didn't want him to go. My dad had died only two weeks before, and I was totally terrified of being left alone so soon. We weren't living together, but Robert had been sleeping on my couch since Dad had passed to keep me company. But he had to go. He had to work, you know?"

She paused to take a sip of tea and collect her thoughts. "I thought I might go crazy if I just sat there and stared at the walls until he got back. Then I remembered that we had found my mom's sewing stuff when we had been putting Dad's things into storage. I went and found her machine, a pattern that I thought would fit me, and some really out-of-date fabric, and I started making a dress."

Peter looked confused, but he just sipped his coffee and nodded his head in encouragement.

She took another sip of tea, then continued. "Robert always used to joke that the only reason he was marrying me was so he could finally see me in a dress. I was a real tomboy, you see. My dad had never minded, and neither had Robert, but I thought I would surprise him."

Her mouth twisted as the memory of that horrible night flooded over her.

Peter looked like he wanted to say something, but he stopped himself, honouring his word.

She smiled gratefully. The next bit was the hard part.

"I got the dress done in time, but the night before Robert was supposed to come home, he called and told me that the airline had rearranged his schedule, and he would be coming home a day later than planned. I pouted and fussed, not wanting him to stay away one moment longer than necessary. The next morning he texted that he was about to get on a plane—he had managed to rearrange his schedule again and was catching a ride home on another pilot's flight. He would be home that night after all."

Pause.

"Only, he wouldn't."

Her voice cracked. "I was getting ready to meet him when I found out that the plane had gone down." She clutched her mug with white-knuckled fingers, eyes moistening.

Peter leaned forward and rested his elbows on his knees. "The article said that it was a mechanical failure. It was not your fault."

Melinda took a deep breath and nodded. "I know. At least, I do now. But I have blamed myself for years for Robert even being on that flight. If I hadn't wanted to see him so badly and made such a fuss, he would have come home the next day and we would have been happily married five weeks later."

She had expected to break down in tears right

then, and was surprised that she had gotten through this confession without her heart being squeezed in the familiar vise-grips of guilt and shame. A surprising calm filled her spirit, and she felt the Father's presence envelop her in peace.

It wasn't your fault, my child.

She exhaled in silent acknowledgement and gratitude.

"Was that when you began designing your dresses?" Peter asked, breaking the silence.

"Yes."

She sighed, gazing backward in time, not at the man before her.

"I didn't want to see anyone, talk to anyone, or do anything for several weeks. For some reason I can't even explain, one day I went and dug out my mother's entire fabric stash and started putting a dress together. When it was finished, I pretended that Robert and I were going on a date, and I told him everything that I had been needing to say to him and couldn't.

"It helped, a little. But—don't laugh at me, but after Robert died, and Mom and Dad had already . . . Well, I . . . I was terrified I must be cursed."

She glanced up to see his reaction, but was met only by a look of intense concern, not a hint of mockery or amusement in his face.

"I was afraid to let anyone else help me, in case they got hurt, too. So eventually, other people stopped even trying. I always managed to close the door on everyone, but only two people refused to stop knocking. Robert's sister Nadia . . . and you."

Peter's bottomless black eyes were burning into her soul, filled to the brim with compassion, and something else she couldn't—or daren't—name. She couldn't bear it, and her gaze fell onto her tea mug instead. She set it on the coffee table, then regained her resolve and looked up at him, silently imploring him to understand.

"I was trying to protect you, Peter. Everyone who ever loved me has ended up dead." She started shivering and wrapped her arms around herself to try to control the shaking. "I thought if I really loved you, I would have to push you away."

At those words, the dam made up of all the lies she had told herself for the last three years crumbled, and she started shaking with sobs. She cried for her father, and for Robert, and for all the scars she thought would never heal. As she cried, the tears washed away all the pain she had held in for so long.

Peter came and put his arms around her, enveloping her in heat and safety and security, shushing her gently as the flood rushed through her. He didn't let go until she had finally stopped shaking and her tears subsided to the occasional sniffle. Then he pulled back a little to look in her eyes, cupping her chin in his hand.

"Melly, I am so sorry for everything you have been through. But it's okay, now. You're here, I'm here, and I'm not going anywhere."

"Wha—what?" she said, trying to dab at her face with a tissue. "What about Vancouver?"

"Silly girl," Peter said, smiling and stroking her hair.

Melinda smiled, too, at the way he said "gull."

"I was only going there because I couldn't bear to be here without you. I'll even go to Toronto, if that's what you want. I'm sure I can find things to take pictures of there."

"You mean you don't want to put in for a transfer with UPS?" She smiled weakly at her attempt at a joke, and then hiccupped.

He laughed, brushing away the last few tears from her cheeks. His touch was like balm on her starved soul. She stared at him, barely daring to breathe, his face only inches from hers. Then he gently pressed his lips against hers.

She welcomed the kiss. It felt like coming home.

"I love you so much," he whispered.

Their lips met again. Electricity crackled into every extremity of Melinda's body, and tears started tracking her cheeks once more.

"What's the matter?" Peter asked, pulling back in concern.

Melinda shook her head, saltwater dripping onto

her tongue past her wide smile. "I never thought I would be this happy again."

He shook his head and clucked his tongue in mock exasperation.

"Cry when you're sad, cry when you're happy . . . I will never in all my life understand women."

She laughed and hiccupped again, which made them both giggle even more.

"You don't have to understand them all," she teased shyly. "Just me."

His arms surrounded her once more. He kissed her firmly, then held her close. She melted into his chest.

"That's a challenge I will gladly take on," he murmured into her hair.

Melinda held him as tightly as she could, her head resting on his shoulder. She breathed in his scent—fabric softener and musk—and her spirit breathed in the safety, security, and freedom of being loved.

She wasn't alone anymore. And she wasn't cursed. And Peter *loved* her.

It was December outside the window. But in her soul, spring had arrived.

It was a long time before either of them relaxed their embrace and pulled away.

"THERE is something else I need to do today," Melinda said at last, "and I was hoping you might agree to come with me."

"What is that, my love?" Peter said and his heart warmed. He could hardly believe that he could use that endearment with her at last.

Her head was on his chest and her hand rested on his thigh. He stroked her hair with one hand and traced the paths of her fingers with the other. The events of the last hour seemed so surreal, Peter felt as though he were floating in the upper ionosphere somewhere. *Except warmer,* he noted to himself with an inward grin.

"Robert's family is holding a private remembrance party this afternoon. I haven't seen any of them in over two years, and I want to go. Once, they were my family, too." She hesitated. "Um, it would mean a lot if you would come with me. Would that be too weird for you?"

"Of course not. I would love to go." He lazily caressed her cheek. "When do we need to leave? And where are we going?"

"They live in Brooks, a little town an hour or so east of here." She twisted her head to look at him with an unreadable expression. "If we catch a cab to the Greyhound station now, we should get there just in time."

"What, *now*?" Peter jumped up. "I'm hardly dressed for the occasion. I haven't even eaten breakfast yet!"

Melinda giggled and held up her two thumbs and forefingers, crossed to make a rectangle with Peter in the middle of the frame. "Click. Gotcha!"

He stared at her, working through what had just happened. "Did you just . . . ?"

She giggled again, biting her lip.

"Why, you little . . ." He laughed out loud.

Melinda laughed, too, and he warmed to see her looking so happy.

"It's good to hear you laugh." He laid a hand on her cheek. Then he stepped back and cocked his head. "That's a pretty dress. Did you make it?"

"Of course I did. I made it to surprise you." She gave a mincing curtsy. "But seriously, we need to leave in about an hour. I'll fix you some toast and eggs while you go change your socks."

He looked down at his mismatched footwear and laughed again. "Sounds good," he said, already heading toward the bedroom. "But I think we'll take my car, if that's okay with you."

"A vehicle. Right. Why don't we take your car?"

He chuckled as he left the room. He could hear the cupboard doors rattling as she hunted down a frying pan.

Maybe they didn't even need the car. He was pretty sure that this morning, he could fly.

Chapter 15

AND NOW, BY THE power vested in me, I pronounce you husband and wife," said Pastor McKay proudly.

Peter was already leaning toward his new bride with the biggest grin of his life when the pastor added "You may kiss your bride."

After wasting no time obeying Pastor Ralph's orders, Peter and Melinda broke apart to cheers from the gathered friends and family. They walked down the cobblestone aisle between white folding chairs on green, fresh grass, both of them sure this was the happiest moment of their entire lives. Their beaming smiles tried to take in each guest as they led the procession out of the gazebo.

They were cheered on by all their favourite people—Peter's parents and grandparents and more of his uncles and aunts and cousins than Melinda had expected to make the trip across the globe. There was Fred, and Sandra and her family—and, in the row in front of them, Edwin and Valerie Clarkson. Nadia and her husband, Jason, marched in the wedding procession behind the bride and groom.

Melinda nodded to as many as she could, looking forward to greeting them all personally at the reception in the large white tent on the other side of the expansive lawn.

She couldn't believe how well the day had worked out. She and Peter had wanted the wedding to be simple, and since Peter's family was also Christian, being married by Pastor McKay was the natural choice.

While the wedding was mostly Western in tradition, they had managed to incorporate some Eastern flair. Red and gold embroidery accented Melinda's flowing white damask silk gown—which she had designed herself, of course—and matched the gold embroidery on the jacket hem and sleeves of Peter's Asian-cut white suit. Both the bride and groom wore a garland of red flowers around their necks, and the heady aroma the flowers gave off moved with them like a cloud of perfume.

Despite the Indian tradition of inviting nearly everyone the couple—and the parents of the couple—knew to a wedding, they had managed to convince Peter's parents that a small gathering was best in this case. Melinda was thankful for more reasons than just financial ones—the minimal stress of the wedding preparations had allowed her to spend some time getting to know her new in-laws better since their arrival from Mumbai several days before.

Of course, not much of the wedding stress had been hers to deal with, anyway. Preeti had Bonnie, her mercenary assistant, plan the wedding. The woman had made sure the whole event ran like a well-oiled machine. Melinda could see Bonnie now, standing behind the last row of chairs, continually scanning to make sure everything was proceeding exactly as it should.

So much had changed in Melinda's life in the six months of her and Peter's whirlwind courtship and engagement. Not least surprising was that she and Preeti had become fast friends. It had begun after Melinda had gone to Preeti for advice on how to go about establishing herself as an independent designer in the Canadian market, and before long they were going shopping, having tea, and hanging out together on a regular basis.

Melinda glanced back at the glowing Indian woman who followed behind her and Peter in the wedding procession and smiled when their eyes met. Preeti smiled back, then glanced down to steady herself as her heels caught on the edge of a cobblestone—her baby bump was quite pronounced now, and she was still getting used to the difference in her centre of gravity. Preeti's husband Michael, who had stood up for Peter, stiffened his arm to give her more stability.

As the wedding party lined up to greet their guests in a traditional receiving line, Nadia wrapped Melinda in a huge hug, tears of joy running down the Matron of Honour's face.

"I know we aren't technically sisters, but I'm as proud of you as if we were. And so very happy. Peter is one of the good ones. Congratulations."

Melinda returned the hug gratefully. "Thank you for always being my friend and never giving up on me, Nadia," she said, tears filling her eyes as well.

With a smile, they stepped into their places as the first guests arrived to shake their hands and wish them well.

"Well, Peter, you managed to get a weekend off, did you?" Edwin Clarkson teased as he shook the groom's hand.

Reuniting with Robert's family had been one of the biggest blessings to Melinda—they had re-adopted her as their own daughter, and had tested and accepted Peter with all the good-natured teasing of incorporating an extra son into the family. Edwin had even given Melinda away.

"Yes, well, I figured it might be a bit awkward to be the photographer at my own wedding," Peter jested back, clasping hands and exchanging gruff hugs with the tall, thin man.

Peter had been able to walk away from his delivery job several months before. He now filled most Saturdays with capturing other people's wedding memories, which supplemented the nearly full-time work he had with *Fresh* and his own expanding home studio clientele.

Melinda glanced proudly at her new husband—*my husband!*—then hugged Edwin and Valerie.

"You look stunning, my dear," said Valerie, eyes twinkling beneath greying brown hair. "And you, young man," she said, taking on a mock scolding tone as she turned back to address Peter. "Take good care of this girl, or you shall have me to answer to."

"Well, I wouldn't want to risk that," Peter grinned. "Don't worry, Mrs. C., I'll have her barefoot and pregnant in no time."

A step behind Valerie, Peter's mother's mouth fell open in shock at the comment. Preeti leaned over and smiled at her mother reassuringly.

"Don't worry, Mama. Peter is only joking—I think he has been spending a little too much time around these redneck Albertans." She fixed her brother with an intense glare. "You were only teasing, right, Peter?"

"Of course I was," he laughed, hands raised in mock defence. "What kind of unsophisticated swine do you take me for?"

Mavis Surati looked only slightly mollified, and rattled off something in Hindi that made Peter put on a chastened look and her husband and Preeti laugh out loud.

"Yes, Mama. I will," said Peter, squeezing the short, plump Indian woman in the glittering sari tightly before extending his hand to his father.

Melinda caught Peter's eye with a questioning glance, but he just gave a subtle shake of his head and grinned sheepishly.

"Melinda," said Mavis with a wide smile, holding her new daughter-in-law's arms in ring-bedecked hands. "I am so glad to welcome you to our family. I can't wait to get to know you better, but from what I have seen so far, I know Peter couldn't have made a better choice."

"Thank you, Mama," said Melinda.

Mavis swooped in for a hug that completely flattened the garland around her neck.

As the procession continued, Melinda floated in a tangerine haze. To have gone from diner waitress to up-and-coming designer—with her own online store, a couple of professional seamstresses assembling her designs, and preparations for her first New York Fashion Week show underway—was nothing short of amazing.

But to have gone from such utter aloneness to having not one, but two families to call her own in so short a time—several friends among them—was enough to make her tremble with joy.

While she didn't expect the rest of her life to be painless and trouble-free, she basked in this moment of complete contentment, soaking in every drop. She also had a calm assurance in her heart that she would never again be alone, planted there when she had visited Pastor McKay last December. God had made her this promise before she was even born, but it was only in that quiet sanctuary that she had finally understood and embraced it.

Peter's hand settled momentarily on the small of her back in a brief moment between well-wishers. She shot him an adoring smile.

Out of the corner of her eye, she thought she caught a familiar face and turned back toward the line in surprise. Standing just beyond the queue of slowly moving guests, across the lawn toward the gazebo, stood her father grinning widely, his grey eyes glinting. One of his arms was around her mother, young and radiant in her favourite plum-coloured dress, and the other was around Robert in his captain's uniform, who smiled and blew a kiss at her. Tears of joy, not sorrow, filled her eyes. She smiled and waved back, and then the image was gone.

No, she didn't know what adventures the next chapter of her life would bring—but for the first time in years, she was eager to find out.

Dear Reader

Thank you for reading *The Friday Night Date Dress*. I hope you enjoyed it as much as I enjoyed writing it. Since this was my first published story, it will always hold a special place in my heart. And this new, revised version finally lives up to the vision I held for this book all along. (What a difference five years can make!)

I'd like to invite you to join my monthly newsletter, in which I talk about Books & Inspiration, usually together. You can also see what's new with my writing, and of course, you can unsubscribe at any time. (You get a free novella as a thank you for signing up!) Sign up at www.talenawinters.com/contact.

Reviews are essential for indie authors to get the word out. If you have a few minutes, I'd really appreciate if you would review this book on the online platform of your choice. It only takes a couple of sentences to make a big difference! (Get direct links here: www.talenawinters.com/friday-night-date-dress.)

If you enjoyed this book, you may also enjoy my romantic psychological fiction novel, *Finding Heaven*, another story of redemptive love about a woman recovering from an abusive past with the help of a humanitarian who works with sex trafficking victims in Mumbai. See more about the book at www.talenawinters.com/finding-heaven.

Thank you so much for reading! It's readers like you that make this writing thing so worthwhile.

Spread sunshine!

Talena Winters
June 2015
Amended June 2020

About Finding Heaven

SOMETIMES TO FIND HEAVEN, you have to go through hell…

Sarah Daniels seems to have the perfect life—a successful career as an erotica author, a successful lawyer husband, thousands of adoring fans, and the freedom to do whatever she wants. Or does she?

Behind the façade, her marriage is a shambles, she hates her career, and she feels trapped behind masks of her own making. A cancer diagnosis has just dealt the final blow to the shaky foundations of her life.

A chance encounter with Steve McGuire—a man who gave up the rat race to help Mumbai's prostitutes and who finds joy in every little thing—makes her question her priorities and wonder if it's time for a change. Like a guardian angel, he keeps helping her pick up the pieces, but the kind of love he offers seems both unrealistic and unattainable. Besides, beneath his easygoing smile, she knows he's hiding something, just like everyone else.

Is it too late for Sarah to find heaven?

Finding Heaven is a gripping, hope-filled story about healing, second chances, and redemptive love.

"A riveting, true-to-life tale of love's power to heal and redeem." - Melissa Keaster, author of *Eleora*

"One of the most beautifully written books I have read." - Kristin Dyck, editor of *Mile Zero News*

Find out more and where to buy at
www.talenawinters.com/finding-heaven.

Acknowledgements

I OWE MANY PEOPLE a debt of gratitude that this book exists.

To my husband, who endures my many nights in front of the computer, listens to me bounce ideas off of him, and even reads my manuscripts (even though he doesn't usually read romance novels), thank you.

To the readers of my blog, Winters' Day In, who have encouraged me to write fiction, thank you.

To my beta readers—my mom, Laurel Easton, and my late friend Laverna Stanley, who have both been unwavering supporters of my writing career, thank you.

To Holly Lisle and Kristen Lamb, whose passion to help writers succeed and teachings gave me the confidence and tools I needed to take the leap, thank you.

To Lora (www.editsbylora.com), my editor,

formatter, and writing coach for the first version of this book—your kind and encouraging words and coaching were invaluable. Thank you for taking my book from good to great, and being good-natured about the American/Canadian "language barrier."

And to you, my readers—thank you for reading my story. I hope you have come to care for Peter and Melinda as much as I do.

About the Author

TALENA WINTERS is addicted to stories, tea, chocolate, yarn, and silver linings. She writes page-turning fiction for teens and adults in multiple genres, coaches other writers, has written several award-winning songs, designs knitting patterns under her label *My Secret Wish*, and is lead writer for *Move Up* magazine. She currently resides on an acreage in the Peace Country of northern Alberta, Canada, with her husband, three surviving boys, two dogs, and an assortment of farm cats. She would love to be a mermaid when she grows up.

You can find her on the web at
www.talenawinters.com.

www.ingramcontent.com/pod-product-compliance
Lightning Source LLC
Chambersburg PA
CBHW011213190726
48288CB00013B/3435